T0147519

Deep Code

Christie W. Kiefer

iUniverse, Inc.
Bloomington

Deep Code

iUniverse books may be ordered through booksellers or by contacting:

iUniverse
1663 Liberty Drive
Bloomington, IN 47403
www.iuniverse.com
1-800-Authors (1-800-288-4677)

ISBN: 978-1-4620-2559-6 (sc)
ISBN: 978-1-4620-2565-7 (hc)
ISBN: 978-1-4620-2566-4 (e)

Printed in the United States of America

iUniverse rev. date: 6/14/2011

Prologue

I write this from my cell in the district prison near Guayaquil, Ecuador. My real name is Morse Brulay. I can tell you that now, because the authorities know, but many people across the Americas still know me by the name of Carlos Bolaños. The pseudonym, and the jail cell, came about because five years ago I made the terrific misjudgment of setting out to learn the Deep Code. A misjudgment is not necessarily a mistake—in fact, this particular misjudgment was probably the only thing that could have torn me loose from a life I now recognize was meaningless—the life of a psychology professor at a small college in San Francisco, teaching my seminars and dabbling in my research on occult states of mind. The life that the Deep Code forced me into, through a twisted path of terror, despair, and discovery, is as deeply rewarding as it is precarious, landing me in a permanent insecurity that would have scared the shit out of me if I could even have imagined it back then.

Over these past three years my partner, Lotte, and I have quietly built an organization called OCA—Otro Camino Arriba—a name that is becoming an everyday word on hundreds of tongues, not just in the bustling streets of Guayaquil, but along the winding narrow paths of the Andes as well. What does OCA mean? Our organization does something that sounds simple and harmless if I say it briefly, but in truth is so revolutionary that we must constantly disguise it in order to avoid persecution: OCA unites and empowers the keepers of the world's indigenous ancestral knowledge. You might expect to find that phrase in the pamphlet of a New Age cult, or a brochure on eco-tourism, but I assure you, what it means in our hands is something altogether different, something so threatening to the keepers of global power that I must mystify it and ourselves to stay alive. But in order for you to understand this, I must take you with me on the bizarre journey that brought us together, drove us into hiding, and gave birth to this fragile and deeply necessary enterprise.

If the words "indigenous ancestral knowledge" mean anything at all to you, they probably conjure up ideas about colorful herbal healers, prescribing their bundles of dried leaves in the markets of remote tropical villages, or shamanic soul doctors, chanting incantations over smoky fires in the jungle night. Or perhaps you think of primitive ways of living that sustain a natural environment, the low technologies of spear and palm thatch that for thousands of years have left scarcely a footprint on the green forest carpet or the desert sand. You would be right, up to a point. The knowledge OCA cultivates includes all this, but it is vastly deeper, a way of knowing you probably cannot imagine, a way that makes the civilized world around you recoil and mutter about insanity.

How can I begin to describe it to you? Let's start with a small slice of this knowledge, the concept of time. You probably believe that the present moment of your life is the product of a fixed past—a past that might be partly remembered or recorded, but that can never be actually relived. You probably consider the details of your future unknowable. I used to think this way too. But there is another way of knowing time, a way that reveals wonderful secrets about ourselves and our universe. In the right state of mind, a state the ancient teachers could access, time can be clearly seen as an open plane that includes what has been and what will be. I'd like to pass the secret of this mind-set on to you if I could; but the truth is, all I can do is describe the process of my learning. You will see that the cost of this knowledge is severe; and that I'm convinced it's worth the cost.

A "time machine" is one of those cartoon concepts that no sensible person takes seriously, and neither do I. But your own mind is capable of transcending time in way most people now can't imagine. I even have to qualify the word "mind." We're familiar with the idea that memory and anticipation are located in our brains, but this is highly misleading.

Our idea of a mind is already located *within* our idea of time, and the one cannot explain the other. If there were a verb for knowing time—let's say, *to timenate*—it would not be our mind which timenates, but something greater which timenates our minds and everything else—but, look, I'm getting ahead of myself.

Chapter One

The Conklin

When I made this great miscalculation I was, as I said, a professor of psychology at a small but reputable college. I didn't much like the institution or the faculty, many of whom struck me as clannish and arrogant. The lab guys—physicists and chemists—had a sense of humor but oozed complacency about almost everything, especially their superiority over the literary and social science types. The latter, when they weren't trying to ruin each other's careers, struggled to instill in their students an overweening reverence for their hangdog cultishness. All this somehow gave the university administration an inflated idea of both the social standing and the moral superiority of our little institution.

It bored the shit out of me. I tolerated it ill-humoredly for the chance to pursue my passion: the study of unusual states of consciousness, especially the way shamans, or "witch doctors," use these unusual states in their work. My critics liked to say this wasn't just an interest in my case, it was an obsession, and point out that I once spent a bit of time in the locked ward of a mental hospital. But that's another story. I knew the clinical definition of obsession, and it didn't fit my experiments at all. They were the result of careful, conscious choices by a highly trained mind. I even enjoyed the tingle of controversy that such accusations lent to my name—Professor Morse Brulay, the madman.

A shaman's job is to acquire and apply useful knowledge of the sort we cannot get in ordinary states of consciousness. The trances, ecstasies, frenzies, and possessions they use to attain it look and sound chaotic to the uninitiated, but this is an illusion. There is an enormous body of knowledge about how to get oneself into these states, and once there, how to control them. The first job of a shaman, or a scientific student of shamanism, is to master this knowledge, and you don't do it by reading books. Before the story I'm about to relate happened, I had sat at the feet of real live witch doctors in New Guinea, Africa, and several Native American communities. When I first heard about the Conklin, the Druid whose knowledge led me into this strange saga, I was confident I could experience what he knew directly, understand it intellectually, and file it away with the rest of my hefty store of lore that goes by such names as the paranormal, the occult, gnosis, magic, or the supernatural. The discovery that I was wrong proved much more enlightening than the object of my original quest.

Domhain comharthai, literally "deep language," or Deep Code, refers to the language that is used in the alternative universe the Druids call *sidh,* the realm of the dark spirits, or *fomors.* I had heard about it now and then over the years, but I would have gone on happily thinking it was a bit of lost knowledge if it hadn't been for my teenage daughter, Thelly. Thelly lives with her mother in Denver, but she's as fascinated with these things as I am. One day I got an e-mail from her, saying she had found a Web site that actually listed masters of various Druidic arts. She drew my attention to a character called the Conklin, who the site said was adept in Deep Code. This was too much of an enticement to resist, and as soon as my spring classes were over, off to Galway I went.

My troubles began at once. Although the Web listing—a footnote from an obscure book on Druidism—said the Conklin lived in the town of Galway, it turned out that he didn't really live in any particular place but practiced his trade throughout Ireland in a seminomadic way, turning up wherever people needed a Druid, and leaving as soon as he was called somewhere else. Worse than that, he seemed to have stopped plying his trade a few years earlier. Although plenty of people had heard of him, or even seen him, they all told me he hadn't been around lately.

But find him I did, no thanks to six strenuous weeks, at least seventy-five drinking establishments, and a veritable Lough Corrib of Guinness pints. In a bar called the Moss Beard, in Limerick, I was introduced by a bartender to a tiny man with an actual beard down to his knees who claimed that the Conklin was a fake, and that he himself was the only true practitioner of the Deep Code. I might have believed him had he not got drunk and tried to recite some of the myths, in the process calling the father of the swan lover Angus "the sun god Belanos," whereas any Druid would have known him as the son of the great and good father-god, Dagdá.

I got a scare in Dingle, where two people independently told me that the Druid had been fingered as an IRA strategist and arrested in Belfast, but further inquiries convinced me that the arrested man had only been using "the Conklin" as a code name.

The pale-eyed proprietress of a bed-and-breakfast near Kinsale told me she had also studied Druidism and knew for a fact that the *domhain comharthai* was pure blarney, dreamed up by an enterprising group of Wiccans in America. "There's a thousand such fairy tales, Perfesser," she said, winking broadly. "Findin' the real teachin' is like lookin' fer mussels at high tide."

I began to despair, wondering if this might go on until the summer was over. But on the twenty-first of July, luck brought me one of those miraculous improbabilities that the Irish seem to take for granted as a feature of everyday life. A telephone operator in Galway told me matter-of-factly that there were forty-two people named Conklin in the local directory, and added as an aside that at this moment he happened to know the exact location of the Druid I was searching for.

I was skeptical, of course, but what could I do but follow up? That afternoon I found myself up to my ankles in mud, a thick mist swirling around me, talking to a goat. Or rather, talking over a goat to a soft voice whose owner wouldn't show himself. The goat eyed me indifferently from the doorway of a dark thatched lean-to against a ruined church outside the small village of Headford. An open grove had grown up in and around the ruin—slender birch, ash, gnarled mossy oaks, tangles of blackthorn and ivy among the fallen stones. It felt beyond odd standing in the middle of this forlorn, forgotten place, trying to explain to a phantom who I was and what I wanted. I told him that I had personal experience with shamanic trance, and that I had come here to learn *domhain comharthai.*

"*Domhain comharthai!* Square wheels and horned virgins! Did the bishop send you, now?"

"Uh, beg your pardon?"

"I tricked the *fomors* into giving me the Deep Code, for the sons of Dagdá are too wise to ever let a mortal have such a thing. The churchmen think I'm a devil. Anyway, whether you're a Christian, a Protestant, or a ghost, you're about five years too late. You can learn it only from the *fomors,* and they have all gone into banking. The *sidhs* are abandoned." This voice was not didactic or dour. It sang. Not melodically, like any music you could identify, but touching an old memory of song, something you heard before you knew what music was. "Out with you, Sheba!" The goat started at the sound of her name and loped past me into the glen.

I knew about the *sidhs.* If there were such a thing as a scientific laboratory, library, cathedral, theater, and enemy stronghold all rolled into one, that would be the modern equivalent of the *sidh* in the ancient Celtic universe. In its complex cosmology there were two main types of spirits—the sons of Dagdá, those of warmth, abundance, sunlight, and life, and the *fomors,* those of cold, scarcity, darkness, and death. These were not opposites, they were partners in a world parallel to the everyday one of our senses, and together they shaped and regulated it. The *sidhs,* usually wild places hidden deep in the forests, were nodes where power and knowledge passed between the underworld of the dark spirits and the human world. A Druid can speak with the spirits almost anywhere, given the proper rites, to diagnose a magic illness, read the future, or cast a spell. But it is to these places of awe and peril, far from the paths of ordinary folk, that he must go to deepen his knowledge and power.

"Banking?" I felt like I needed an interpreter.

"Charming other people's money so it dances into your own pants," the voice said. "There's no advantage in torturing souls the old way, with magic visions and curses and the like. The *fomors* have better things to do, now that everyone's got a job."

"The *sidhs* are abandoned, you said? Have you given up your practice, then?"

"What practice? O' being poor? No, no. When I die I'll be trying to pick the pearls off them gates."

"I mean your teaching, your healing. Don't tell me there's no use for the old knowledge…"

"Well, do I hear an offer? Gimme a pint and I'll tell you the whole Cuchulainn cycle, and throw in a perfectly good hatchet handle."

"I tell you, that's what I'm here for, to learn the lore. Of course I'll pay you."

There was a pause, then, "Come back on *meán foghamar.* There's a Druidic festival here, with lots o' storytelling."

Meán foghamar, the autumn equinox, was two months away. I felt he was testing me, the way shamans do. At any rate, it was preposterous to suggest that I should just go back to San Francisco. "I'm not interested in a Druid festival. I came to see you, because you know *domhain comharthai*. Surely the knowledge is still sound."

"I'll see you on *meán foghamar."* The voice was decisive this time.

There was a gigantic oak tree twenty yards from the doorway, with high, gnarled roots to sit on, and that's where I sat. The hovel door slowly closed. The goat had ambled back to stand on its hind legs and nibble at the edges of the thatch. After a couple of hours the mist cleared, and I could see the slate sky through the black tracery of the ruin's gothic skeleton. The bells of a living church in the distance pealed. I ate one of the energy bars I had brought. The sky gradually faded to black, but I could still feel and smell the stonework, and I saw a faint glimmer of light from the Conklin's lean-to.

I hadn't been able to find much writing about the Deep Code, just enough to get a student of shamanism into a fierce curiosity. It had something to do with mental time travel—exceptionally vivid images of things that happened perhaps hundreds or even thousands of years ago. Of course it was considered witchcraft and heavily suppressed wherever Christianity took over, which tells us it had spiritual power. And of course there were also monks who practiced and wrote about it in their own esoteric ways, before what Yeats called "the evil chance." It was one of the many, many jewels of Irish culture that fell with the tears of the 1840s famine into the rotten clay. But apparently it didn't disappear altogether. A few people in my lifetime claimed to have experienced it, though they didn't write about it or teach it to others. In public they preferred for their own reasons to let others scoff at the idea, lumping it with leprechauns and banshees.

It was barely light when I woke, shivering. As I got up to look for a place to pee, I saw that he—or someone—had left near my perch a cold chicken leg and a glass of something that looked like tea but turned out to be neat whiskey. This might have been highly encouraging, or it might just have been someone's sense of propriety. They say that if you're hungry in Ireland, one of the stones will lay you an egg and another will coddle it for you. There was a tiny kitchen garden next to the hut, with a crude stone well and plastic bucket in the middle of it. Taking care not to step on the tender plants, I drew water, washed, drank, then went back and ate. Now and then I took a small sip of the whiskey, wondering if he was watching, wondering whether this was another test, wondering how long I could sit there, and whether it was futile after all. I tried to imagine what he looked like. His voice sounded neither young nor old, neither that of a large nor a small man. For a moment I had the startling sensation that the hut itself might be a *sidh;* that there was no actual person there, just the disembodied voice of a dark spirit; and even that the goat was the temporary vehicle of that spirit, and that the voice I heard was coming from her. Solitude and boredom do such things to the mind, something I knew well from other shamanic quests.

On the third day there was bread and fruit, but no whiskey. I guessed there must be another door to the hut, inside the ruin maybe, through which he was going in and out without being seen. Late in the afternoon a couple of boys passed near the old stone walls, throwing rocks at the crows. I called to them, gave them a few pounds, asked them to fetch me some sweets and keep the change. As they hurried off I envied them each other's company. A couple of hours later they came back with chocolates and caramels, and the change, which I told them again to keep. They wanted to talk, but I told them to run along. Social recreation shows something other than strength of will. I left the candy at the door of the hut.

The next morning the candy was gone and I wondered if the crows had taken it. I began to be tortured by the idea that he really meant to make me wait two months. How long *would* I actually wait? Why hadn't I brought my herbs and amulets? In a pinch, maybe I could reach the soul-travel level of trance without them, given my long experience. There were plenty of ancestors, gods, and spirits I could call on. I began to sing a New Guinea ancestor song, to breathe it, to feel myself lighten…

I don't know how much time had passed when I felt a presence and looked up to see a figure regarding me from forty feet away. The sun was hidden in low clouds. I was not sure at first whether I was still in full trance and this was a spirit. It looked like a middle-aged farmer of this place—stocky, a bit stooped, in heavy, shapeless clothes, a cigarette in its mouth, hands in its trouser pockets, but without the standard porkpie hat. I nodded to it, and it turned and walked into the hovel. Gradually my senses cleared and I felt the trance lift or, as they say, my soul return to my body. This was probably another test. Either he, or a spirit sent by him, had approached me in trance. He, or it, must know of my uncertainty. What would I find in the hut?

One mustn't rush, one mustn't hesitate, one must be light and easy like leaves in the wind. In the low-watt electric lamp of the lean-to, I saw a strong face, clean shaven, ruddy, gray hair needing a barber, good teeth (false?), an alert, pale right eye and the left one closed by a scar. There was only a cot, a small table, and a couple of stools in the hut.

"You're not from here. Either the police are after you or you used the wrong map." That musical voice. Its owner passed me a loaf of white bread and a knife, indicated a plate of butter, apples, and a pot of tea on the table. The hands were large, quick, and graceful, like a magician's.

"American. My people are originally from France, mostly, five generations back. Could have been Celtic I suppose." Hungry though I was, I was even more afraid of eating this and would have said no if custom hadn't compelled me to accept. I cut a modest slice.

"Celtic? Lock the door and count the children. I can see that might keep you up at night."

"Ancestry is a fine subject, but I haven't thought about it, scarcely at all."

"We wouldn't think of anything else at all here, if it weren't for whiskey and fiddles." Sheba the goat wandered in and stood nodding her head sagely.

"Then you must know a lot about it."

"There's one of our mighty sufferings."

"Ah. And what are the others, may I ask?"

"If you're interested you may, but I only have it by hearsay, mind you."

"I can see that, but tell me anyway."

"Not on an empty stomach, though."

Bread and butter and fruit, gulps of tea. The food seemed real enough. While we talked about New Guinea, and how it changed my life, the one eye took my measure, and I self-consciously reflected on what it saw: a man of fifty, hawk-nosed, tall and athletic, balding, glasses. Levis, leather jacket, canvas backpack, black computer bag with my laptop in it. What does anyone read when they look at us? I waited for a mention of the purpose of my visit, but none came.

"I know it's dangerous to enter a *sidh,"* I finally said. "I'm familiar with dark spirits. Of course I know I might be talking with one right now. I take responsibility for that, you see."

Smiling now, he reached over to the wall where a shard of mirror hung, took it down, and held it next to his face at such an angle that I could see his reflection and know that he was not a spirit.

We talked for perhaps two hours. He insisted that what he had told me about abandoned *sidhs* was true. "In the old times, when we were all so poor the judge had to sing for his supper, the *fomors* could easily lure souls with a scrap o' gold or a clean maid, catch them with riddles, cheat them out o' everything down to their pig's grunt. Now, don't you see, any boy o' five can lend you his smoking jacket, and with a watch in each pocket. No, the Dark Folk are up with the times. You'll find 'em on the twenty-first floor. No offense to me good Sheba, there, but they hide their cloven hoofs in Italian kid."

"Is no one at all interested the Deep Code, the *domhain comharthai*, then?"

A misty look came over him. "'Twas never necessary to learn the Deep Code in order to converse with the *fomors.* Ever since the high laurels of wizardry passed to the lads of the cross, most Druids were satisfied with an apprentice level—to learn the sacrifices, the herbs, the songs, and the trances that might unseal the lips of those who gave and withheld life, who knew the past and future and saw the far away."

"But you have studied their true language?"

"Plain folk speak of the Deep Code as a language," he said, "but that's not how it is. Those who know it don't need to talk to the spirits. They can see the world as the Dark Ones see it, from outside of time."

"Outside of time?"

"That's how it is."

"They can travel back and forth in time, then?"

"Back and forth? South and north? A sailor's prick doth point the course? Most folk can't think of time any way but 'back and forth,' like it was the thread off a spinning wheel. You know about transmigration?"

"The re-birth of souls? Of course, every culture knows of it."

"There. You're a learned man, but no. 'Re-this,' and 're-that' means to come back, to do something over again. In truth, the birth and what you call the rebirth, they're one event, not two."

"Cyclical time. The Hindu Vedas."

"Cyclical is for circus bears. Have a peanut but not the fingers please. You don't make time into a wheel."

"Everything exists at the same time, then?"

"Can you visualize it?"

"No."

"That's the Deep Code."

"How do you get to it?"

"Like I said, the *sidhs* are vacated, closed for the duration. You might catch a *fomor* there on *meán foghamar.* They're sentimental, don't y' see."

"Will you teach me what you know?"

His one eye inspected my two. He shook his head. "I'm sorry, I cannot be the one. If the *sidh* near here, Cuimhne, is forsaken by the *fomors,* there's no reason to go there. If it's not, well, you'll be throwing dice for your soul, playing Irish pinochle, y' might say, where your arse is the Peg-Board and they've a stacked deck."

I heard the slightest hesitancy in his voice. I jumped to my feet. "You can't be the one? Chicken farts! What do *you* do when the only spirit who knows a thing won't talk?"

A grin spread slowly across his marred face. "I try another trick! Your brain has the Druid's pox, it has! Now I'm sure your soul was out sightseeing when I found y' this afternoon, certainly 'twas. Come back tomorrow, then."

We stepped outside. I was surprised I hadn't noticed before that the grove had a powerful smell, a sweet sourness of sap and wet grass and black earth. The smell flung me back to my early childhood, some moment when I had stood in such a grove and imagined the crouching presence, the glowing eyes, of wildness. This image stayed with me on my hour's walk to the Headford Inn.

Chapter Two

The Sidh

He was a natural teacher. We spent the first day testing my ability to memorize prayers, songs, the names of herbs and holy objects, the steps of rituals. Since shamanic knowledge often depends on spirit travel, he made sure I had mastered the trance state for it. He quickly saw that these were skills I had honed over years as a student of the paranormal, and the arduous training started. He told me we were going to search out the *fomors,* wherever they might be, for only they could give me the key to the Deep Code. This would be a foolhardy adventure until I had learned the habits and personalities of the most important spirits. We must study as well their animal familiars—the otter, the crow, the bull, the boar, the hart, along with the lore of the particular place we would visit, Cuimhne. There are no textbooks on any of this; the knowledge is woven into the great oral encyclopedia of the Celtic myths. I had studied what this or that scholar had written down, but there were of course huge gaps in my knowledge. In the following weeks—as my excitement and impatience grew—the Conklin labored to discover these gaps and at least paper them over with the rudimentary facts. I entered everything on my laptop, then uploaded it to my Web site so I could access it with my iPhone. Time passed quickly. Between lessons we would drink tea, while he played the harp prettily.

Meán foghamar, the autumn equinox, September twenty-first, is the time when the *fomors* are most active, preparing to bring winter's cold bareness back to the ripe fields and buzzing green woods. On September eighteenth the Conklin made a kit containing herbs and a small knife, led me to the hill above the ruined church, and pointed west over Lough Corrib. On the far distant banks, we could see the dense forest called Conamara, "descendant of the sea," which hid our destination, the once great and terrible *sidh* of Cuimhne. "I'd sooner bet we'd find an archbishop in this here church ruin," he said, "but y' never know with the *fomors.* If they'll be there a-tall, this is the time."

As darkness fell there on the hill, he built a small fire, on which he laid the herbs, whose names and uses I now knew well: brooklime (to open the third eye), mandrake and its sister selfheal (protection against spells), and mistletoe (the student's friend). He had a small gourd of the blue paint Druids make from the woad bush and, ordering me to strip naked, in silence he painted my legs and feet—including the soles—my lower body and genitals, and my left hand with it. He did the same to himself. He then pierced my right forearm lightly with the knife, dipped a twig in my blood, and wrote a runic cipher on a slip of birch bark from his kit. Holding this up he said, "You shall be called *Ar-thine,* 'burning,' and I need not tell you why." He placed the bark on the fire. "Get dressed. Our work is done. We rest until *meán foghamar.*"

I stayed away from the hut for the next two days, alternately walking alone in the stony hills and meditating in my hotel room, silently rehearsing what I had learned in the last weeks. On the twentieth we packed blankets, bread, and fruit. To his kit the Conklin added herbs and a brick of pork fat wrapped in a white cloth tied with willow strips, and another bundle that looked like a rolled up deerskin. He handed me a large leather water pouch with a shoulder strap and a neck of bone. Just in case, I brought my iPhone along as well. We set off in the morning for Conamara, as the *sidh* was a day's walk from Headford.

For most of the way there was an open footpath around the edge of the lake, now and then cutting into the forest where there were buildings by the water's edge. We were glad for the cool shade, as the sun was strong. On the morning of the twenty-first we rose before daybreak from our bedrolls in the woods and climbed a small hill, where the Conklin offered herbs and prayers to the rising equinoctial sun. For an hour we followed a path that had been trodden deeply into the boggy soil by centuries of feet, then turned off it into the deep woods and our pace slowed as we pushed through thickets and climbed over gnarled roots and boulders. I could not see any path or markers now, but the Conklin seemed sure of the direction.

The shafts of sunlight filtering down through the trees were vertical when he finally stopped and sat down on a rock. "Cuimhne is just ahead," he whispered. "Remember, you must do the talking if we meet anyone. Do you have all of it?"

"The spirits will use enticements and tricks to get hold of my soul, but if I follow the Druidic rules, I may trick them into giving me the Deep Code. Answer their questions with questions, and don't speak my name or any human name or place. Don't fall asleep. Touch things only with my feet and left hand. Don't eat or drink anything, or take anything away from the *sidh.* If I feel an itch or any other sensation in my body, or get an erection, ignore it. If I feel fear, anger, or sorrow, remain calm at all costs. If I feel the urge to move my bowels, or to cry out, or to run, resist it by all means. If I cannot control myself, or simply want to end the journey, immediately call '*tarrthail Danán,*' so the goddess Danán will bring my soul back to my body."

"And what do the *fomors* crave above all?"

"To be remembered forever, with prayers and sacrifice. If I recognize them, call them by their mythic names; if I don't know the name, I say 'Elathan.'"

We came to a stream, where he filled the water pouch. A little beyond this, in an area of great twisted oaks and smooth boulders, there was a rise in the forest floor, a hill hidden in the growth. The stillness was so deep that I startled when I heard a leaf fall to the ground fifty feet away; and yet it seemed to be somehow alive, pulsating with energy. The day was warm and bright, but I felt my hands and feet go cold. At the foot of the hill we shed our packs. The Conklin made a circle of small stones and laid bunches of herbs around it at the four compass points. He made a small fire and for at least an hour quietly offered prayers in Gaelic, adding the herbs and fat from his sacred bundle, bit by bit, and then adding the cloth and bark wrapping to the fire. He unrolled the deerskin and, scooping a handful of ashes from the edge of the fire, rubbed it on the smooth side, then rubbed the remainder on our faces.

With a fallen branch he swept earth over the ashes, then beckoned. We went up to the top of the mound, which must have been two hundred feet in diameter and forty feet high, and which I took to be an ancient grave. The summit was isolated within a rough ring of huge stones and trees, and here he spread out the deerskin and we sat cross-legged on it, facing west, the direction of death and the *fomors.* We both began the breathing and mental concentration that lead to spirit journey.

The sun dipped low. I began to have trouble concentrating, and I woke from trance. The Conklin was still in deep trance. I was wondering whether I should try to call him back, when I heard a rustling in the oaks and looked up to see a large owl staring at us. A strange thing, for a night bird to be here now. A strange thing for a master of stealth to draw such attention to himself. I began to tremble and prepared to go into trance again.

The owl took wing, but it had scarcely disappeared than I heard another sound, a mournful baritone voice, singing,

They put me into jail without judge or writin'
For robbing Colonel Pepper on Kilgary Mountain
But they didn't take me fists so I knocked the sentry down
And bid a fond farewell to the jail in Sligo town.

Musha rig um du rum da
Whack fol the daddy o
Whack fol the daddy o
There's whiskey in the jar

From the west the singer stepped into the ring of rocks, an odd character indeed. Thin, pale-skinned, little more than a dwarf, oddly dressed in crisp gray slacks, blue blazer, and cream-colored shirt with a red ascot, a natty snap-brim hat, expensive loafers. He had a well-trimmed head of white hair, but his features were strong, his skin smooth, his movements agile. He approached us without hesitating and sat primly on a stone, crossing his legs.

"D' ye know what day it be?" he smiled.

I glanced at the Conklin and saw that he was still in trance. "The day before tomorrow, and the one after yesterday," I said.

"Aye, an' a century between 'em if yer not careful. What be yer name?"

"Sorry, I left it back at home. To lighten the load, you know."

"We should lend ye a new one, then."

"Neither a borrower nor a lender be. What's your price?"

"Why, lend *us* a name first."

"I should call you Elathan, then."

"Elathan!" he bellowed and, slapping his knee, leaped up and began to dance. "Elathan! Show me yer left paw! Aha! Yes, ye're Druids! We should've known it when we tasted th' smoke o' yer fire!" He sat down again. "Our name's Dryr, now tell us who we are."

"No harm in telling what you already know, younger son of Elffin, that saved the boy Taliesin from the waters."

"And why pass we here?"

"Why? It's *meán foghamar,* and there still might be a sacrifice or two."

"What brings *ye* here to this once fearful, now tearful temple, then? A curse ye're needin' is it? A spell? By Midir, speak an' ye'll have it!"

I was wild to tell him my purpose, but the Conklin's warning stopped me. "What do you call the *fomors'* way of seeing beyond time?" I asked.

"Beyond time? *Domhain comharthai."* His face turned grave. "No, but we mustn't speak o' that. 'Tis a trade secret, ye know."

"Why, you're not a *fomor* at all, are you?"

He folded his arms and cocked his head to one side. "What if we're not?"

"Then I should be off, for I need to find one. I want to tell my children's children that I met an actual *fomor,* and that his name was Dryr. Why should I remember I met an imposter?"

"We're not authorized to speak of *domhain comharthai,* an' that be th' long an' th' little of it," he sniffed.

"And who is?"

"An' what kind o' Druid are *ye* that we should give ye th' dew off our left bollock?" He leaned forward, stared intently into my eyes. I did not blink. "Tell us th' story o' Peredur," he said at length.

I remembered the name Peredur from the Conklin's teaching, but I drew a blank on the story. "Peredur, yes," I felt a tickle of sweat on the back of my neck. I pulled my knees up to my chest, so that my lap was hidden from his gaze, and eased my iPhone from my pocket. I pretended to close my eyes but peeked just enough that I could log on to my Web site and search "Peredur." As soon as I saw the first words of the story I remembered it all. "The knight Peredur passed through a deep valley with a river, and trees on both sides. On one side of the valley white sheep were grazing, on the other side, black. When one of the white sheep would bleat, one of the black would jump in the river and come out white on the other side. When a black sheep would bleat, the opposite. Black to white, white to black."

"That's sixpence worth," he said. "Where's the rest?"

The rest. What the hell was the rest. Oh, yes, yes, the tree. "Peredur saw a tree by the river, half covered with green leaves, the other half with flames."

"And what's the meaning?"

"The transmigration of souls. The river separates the living and the dead. For every birth there is a death, for every death, a birth."

"And the tree?"

"Death and life grow from the same root. The gods of dark and the gods of light, the *fomors* and the race of Dagdá and Danán, are the same."

He nodded slowly, but his face turned grim. "The same race, indeed. But there be a mighty difference, too. Can ye tell me what I'm speakin' of?"

"I'm offering prayers to the *fomors* today, but not to the bright spirits; that's the difference."

"Aye. There were a time," his translucent face now flushed with indignation, "when our mortal children knew the price o' things, from th' tiny to th' terrible. A good song an' dance fer a day o' silver sun or a safe trip through th' bogs of a night fog; an ox fer th' love of one so fair as rapes yer heart. A fat quilt o' barley over th' dale will cost ye th' shrouding of a child; an' glory in th' wet red reaping o' the battlefield, th' promise of a dozen treasured lives. A fortnight for each sacrifice, a shroud o' new white wool, a silver dagger with th' hilt o' ruddy gold. Day an' night from here at Cuimhne an' all th' *sidhs* rose scents o' roasting, sweetened with a hundred lungs o' song. Th' keenest tongues, wordsmiths as could make the sea turn sweet or charm th' moss off holy oaks, fought for th' honor of our ears; aye, an' with th' singin' came as well th' hospitality of queenly thighs. In every burstin' banquet th' biggest bowls brought forth the *fomors'* feast; an' think ye not th' very mice would dare to taste it 'til we'd loosed our buckles wi' th' fill of it. Ours were th' clearest pools, th' stoutest twisted oaks, th' crags still kissed by snow when all th' hills were stony dry; nor would any mortal risk his hand upon 'em 'til he'd paid the fee in poetry. Wizards watched the wandering of our lights on starry nights, an' from a thousand backs there rose a million groans t' lift in place th' hundred granite pillars in each of our thousand cairns and henges. That were all before th' heroes' time."

"The heroes?"

"That rotten mob! Cuchulainn, Medb, an' Conchobar, Cú Roí, an' Emer," he named a few of the thousand mortal demigods of the forty thousand Irish myths. "There was th' work o' th' gods o' light; o' Dagdá an' Danán an' the rest; but ye Druids was as much t' blame, singin' th' tales until th' very stones could repeat 'em til th' last verse. Th' gods o' light have a weakness, y' see, fer th' delights o' mortal society. They'll get mortal births, an' give 'em, at th' drop of a petticoat; then go on an' arm their brats with every privilege o' divinity itself—except the one thing they can't give."

"Immortality," I said.

"An' that's nine fifths o' the wickedness, don't ye see? A hero is a god's child; there's nothin' as rots the mind with pity like yer own child's death; an' there ye have it, a god all soured up with tears an' lame regrets. Now ye're askin' me, I'll enlighten ye that a god like that's no god a-tall! Filth o' fiends! The mortals coddles to 'em so; paints their images all higgledy on every hovel door along with vile Christian saints, an' kneels to kiss the feet o' that."

Shouting now, he jumped up and began to howl, with his fists clenched high above his head, dancing a jig of blind rage, kicking up a cloud of dust, his face a horrible shade of purple, flecks of spit flying from between his clenched teeth. The sight of it put me in such a panic I thought I might wet myself, and I was tempted to call *tarrthail Danán* as the Conklin had advised; but at the same time it occurred to me that at that moment he was cursing my potential savior Danán and her kind, and my prayer might drive him homicidal. The next moment, his fury ended as quickly as it had begun and he sat down.

"One race we are," he went on, calmly, "but no more kin than a gamecock an' a chicken stew."

"I thank you for your teaching, and remember every word. It's we, the Druids after all, who keep you *fomors* in our songs and sacrifices."

"Aye, an' so ye do the simperin' gods o' light, too!" he shook his finger at me.

"Not so as to harm you."

"A *fomor* don't ask *why*," he sneered. "*Why's* the question of a jilted maid. A god asks only *what*, and *how*."

"How, then, can I learn the *domhain comharthai?*"

"*Domhain comharthai,* 'tisn't a game a-tall. Yer soul must cross the river. 'Twill not come back the same." We sat there silently for a moment, and I stealthily pointed the lens of my iPhone in his direction and snapped off four or five shots before he stood up. "Get ye t' th' boardroom of th' Global Progress Group in Dublin." He turned and strode off, his dark silhouette disappearing over the brow of the hill, backlit by the fading western light, singing,

Now some take delight in fishin' and in bowlin'
And others take delight in carriages a-rollin'
But I take delight in the juice of the barley
And courtin' pretty girls in the mornin' so early

Musha rig um du rum da
Whack fol the daddy o
Whack fol the daddy o
There's whiskey in the jar

When the Conklin finally woke from trance it was dark and cold.

The two of us made our way off the hill and as we built a fire, I told him all that had happened. "I felt as though I was awake," I said. "But now I'm not sure."

"We'll find out, won't we? When we get t' Dublin, I mean."

"And where were you all the while?"

"I was watchin' from a ways off," he said, but I could tell from his smile that he was hiding something from me.

"Did you call that *fomor,* Dryr, to meet me?"

"Cut me a haunch o' that soda bread."

"Maybe *you* were Dryr, or maybe there was no such being."

"All we know for sure," he said, "is that this bread's half a day short of blue moldy." He filled his mouth and stared into the fire as he chewed. I suddenly remembered the photos I had taken with my iPhone. I opened it and pushed the display button, half expecting to find that the *fomor* had left no image. My puzzlement actually deepened when I saw him there on my tiny screen—hat, blazer, and all.

Chapter Three

The Trial

In a sense, then, our visit to Cuimhne *sidh* was a success. My performance with the *fomor* yielded good information, the location of the elite Dark Folk who alone could grant access to the *domhain comharthai*. But this was not altogether a happy thought, meaning as it must that my quest had just begun, and the hardest part lay ahead. What did the Conklin know about these modern *fomors,* who wore business suits and worked their dark powers with the help of middle managers? I asked him as we made our way back along the forest trail toward Headford.

"Th' *fomors,* they'll bargain for your soul, they will," he said. "Now there's some things as never change about the work o' catchin' souls. Mortals have five great fears that're never satisfied—the pain o' the flesh, loneliness, shame, death, an' boredom. Those are the engines that drive all our foolishness, for we'll do anything t' be rid o' them.

"What about greed? Lust? Pride?"

"Aye, the medieval trilogy. Greed is just a Mickey Finn, a cocktail o' the fears. We imagine that if we've got ten times what we need, we can quit goin' about searchin' for our next roast o' beef, pint o' Guinness, handshake, or colleen's thighs. Lust? Well, 'tis just the brat sister o' greed, tryin' to dodge loneliness an' boredom. Pride? The fear o' shame, nothin' else. The higher a man rises over the crowd, the farther 'tis to the bottom, an' the more damage he does t' protect his pride. Even the tonsured whiskey pots o' the Church will tell ye 'tis the great sultan o' the sins."

"The threat of death would seem the greatest."

"Aye, but it ain't. Emptiness an' senselessness are other words for death. 'Tisn't life itself we fear t' lose, but the value of things, their meaning, don't ye see? Justice, truth, beauty. Life without 'em 'tis the same as death. Just think o' martyrdom: there's many as will gladly die, or suffer any pains, t' keep what makes 'em *feel* alive."

"What strengths does a man have to bargain with these dark spirits, then? Do they too have fears?"

"Aye. As ye saw back there at Cuimhne, they fear t' be forgotten. That's where a Druid's power lies, in what he remembers, an' the proof he gives of it."

"And how do the modern *fomors* expect to be remembered, then, the ones in the three-piece suits? Do they have their own Druids, their own songs and stories, their own rituals and *sidhs?*"

"Ye can answer that yerself, Ar-thine. What did the Druids do of old?"

"They used their learning to harness the power of nature—the power of the spirits both light and dark—for human ends; to protect the harvest, to ensure success in battle, to cure the sick, to turn danger and misfortune into good luck."

"And what were the armies of their power?"

"Their only strength was guile. Flattery. Riddles. Music. Stories. Magic tricks."

"An' who does that today? Who brings the riches of the boardroom to the service of the poor? Who woos the tinker an' the milkmaid into speakin' the names of the mighty?"

Was he talking about advertising, I wondered. No, the pitch man aims only for money. He was talking about charity. "The financiers have their philanthropies," I said at length. "They endow this or that charity, this or that nonprofit serving the disadvantaged, the voiceless."

"Go on."

"But again, it's the powerful who choose, isn't it? Philanthropy is good public relations. Its main purpose is to deflect dissent."

"And who speaks the truth against those who cloak their selfish aims in sweet pretenses?"

"Who are the Druids of today, you mean?" I turned the question over in my mind. "If the Druids have a modern voice, it's the voice of the dissident, the artist, the satirist, isn't it?"

He was silent, letting his question continue to trouble me. My long admiration of the world's shamans had grown with my knowledge of their personal skill and charisma. I had never turned my attention to their goodness, to what they sacrificed for their communities. In the same vein, all this time I had selfishly thought of *domhain comharthai* as a personal achievement, something to advance my power and my career. What gentle wisdom there was, then, in the Conklin's admonitions. With such a project I could offer nothing to the spirits; why would they offer me anything in return? Would I never learn from the blunders of my egotism? The *fomors* want everlasting admiration. To have it, they can either threaten to destroy, or promise to serve, humanity; and in either case their actions rebound to nature, and themselves. If I wanted the Deep Code, I'd have to convince them I would use it in the service of their fame. What a horrible thought!

Now it appeared that I was caught by my own guile. I had already come too far to give up the quest, and I'd have to accept the burden of it, which I was just now beginning to understand. The Druids flattered their way into the good graces of the *fomors* in order to weaken their power. If I were to serve the values I thought I believed in, the values of human equality and dignity, I must become a Druid, and a Druid is essentially a spy.

We walked in silence for a long time, my mind in turmoil. I had to prepare a proposal to the *fomors*' charity, in this case Global Progress Group, and it had to be the Magna Carta of proposals. I had no idea where to begin. How would my learning the *domhain comharthai* help to memorialize the *fomors,* add to the luster of their names, bring them admirers, erect monuments to them? I had to find a connection between the Deep Code and the admiration of the masses. I had to promise people relief from the five fears the Conklin had spoken of. To my surprise, I began to feel a tremendous determination to do it. Academic life had its challenges after all—to charm the guardians of research money by weaving their favorite incantations into a grant proposal whose result they wouldn't even understand; to turn one's colleagues' ignorance into admiration with a claim so absurd no one had thought of it before. Hadn't I used these and a dozen other bluffs a hundred times each to advance my game?

By the time we arrived back in Headford I had the rough outline of my plan. With access to the Deep Code, one should be able to see specific past events exactly as they had really happened. With this uncanny ability one could claim to help humanity in several ways. Forensics and medicine came immediately to mind, but I had no training in those fields. No, I only had to think of the possibilities in my own field, psychology. Such a gift would not only allow me to reconnect people with forgotten or suppressed memories, it would give me insight into *how* and *why* memory fails, lead to improvements in education as well as psychotherapy. Whatever *fomor* names were lent to this extraordinary new science of memory would become (as would mine) household words, on a plane with Freud, Jung, and William James. It would take money, of course, but a few million was petty change to the modern *fomors.*

I was tremendously excited. I would make them famous, of course; but not the way they thought. A Druid, a spy, I would unleash the Deep Code not simply as their public relations boon, but to help lift up humanity from very ignorance that has always fueled the *fomors'* power to deceive.

It was no problem to locate, via the Internet, the meeting place of the board of directors at the Dublin headquarters of Global Progress Group. Getting personal access to the board would be trickier; but I figured a display of Druidic knowledge would take me a long way toward that. I studied the business news archives and learned that Global Progress Group had major investments in certain European pharmaceutical companies that were now developing psychiatric meds. It owned stock in a chain of elite American chemical and psychiatric rehab centers, and in a gigantic Japanese "nature cure" consortium catering to the families of demented elderly. The *fomors* knew well, then, the value of what I would offer them. Their names would shine forth in the pantheon of mental healers.

I talked the Conklin into letting me get him a cell phone, so he wouldn't have to come with me to Dublin. "Where do I find a wire to hook it to the pole? And where's its damned crank?" he asked.

The real trick, of course, would be to engage at least one of the Global Progress Group directors face to face. With a few hours of searching I managed to come up with press photos of two of them—a rotund, jolly-looking fellow named Winfield Farrell, and a surprisingly pretty fortyish redhead named Dierdre Hynes. I would go to Dublin and arrange to meet these people, somehow.

For now, I was very glad I had taken pictures of the *fomor* Dryr at Cuimhne. I would print copies of these, which I could show the directors as a kind of calling card. I downloaded the photos from my iPhone to my laptop, in order to look at them more closely, and when I did, I saw something that I had not noticed—something far beyond puzzling: the face in the photos was not at all like the face I had seen with my own eyes at Cuimhne. The face I saw there at the *sidh* was delicate and small, active, engaging, the face of an actor or a politician. The one in the photo, there was something wrong with it. Heavy-jawed, heavy-browed, threatening, inward.

"Holy shit!" I said aloud.

The Conklin, who had been fitting a new string to his harp, came and looked over my shoulder. "What in the mad dog night is that?" he said. "Great fires o' hell! Did ye take a photograph of the *fomor* at Cuimhne?!" I turned to him and saw his mouth open, his face a horrible ashen shade. "Did ye forget, then?" he went on, almost shouting, "T' bring anything away from a *sidh,* 'tis t' sign an' seal a curse on the hand as bears it! Did ye bring anything else?"

"Just four pictures, I didn't know..."

"Get rid o' those photographs, all of 'em, quick! Then we'll make sacrifice. Ah, Mother Danán an' all the souls o' Eire!"

I needed the photos for my plan, but I could see it was no use arguing with him in the state he was in. Apologizing the best I could, I immediately deleted them from my computer; but I said nothing about the copies still in my iPhone's memory. Perhaps, I thought, the *fomors* wouldn't know about those either. We took his herb bag and pork fat to the hilltop above his hut, where we had prepared for Cuimhne, and he made a fire and sent prayers to the *fomors,* asking them to lift whatever curse might come to me from my mistake; and to the gods of light as well, asking for protection in case the first prayers failed.

When we got back to the hut, he handed me the cell phone I had given him and stood looking black and funereal. "Morse, ye must go back t' California now. Get off this path, break off this terrible pilgrimage. I take the blame for all of it, I do. I never should've let ye come this far. Ye know a lot about the spirit world, ye do, and I thought we might get away with it, but I was thinkin' with me fool's hat on. Now ye're up to yer tonsils in the devil's privy, and ye've got to get out while ye can."

He hadn't called me Morse since he gave me my Druid name, Ar-thine. I fought back tears. "It's not your fault. I talked you into it, and now I've let you down. You're a great and a kind man, and I took advantage of your kindness, that's all. Forgive me."

He sat silent for a while, then stood and rested his head wearily against the doorpost. "Let's forgive each other, then, but ye must leave Ireland now, an' come back way past never."

"I can't lie to you," I said, "I'm going to Dublin. I take responsibility for everything. Everything. I'm a shaman. I'll make prayers to the *fomors* and the sons of Dagdá."

He turned away and stood for a long time staring out the tiny window of the hut, his arms folded, shoulders hunched. As I watched he slowly relaxed and turned toward me. "Ye're a stubborn man," he said sadly.

In silence we ate a meal of bread and cold canned corned beef, washed down with neat whiskey. I gathered up my things, we shook hands, and I turned to go. "One thing," I said.

"Aye?"

"Can I keep 'Ar-thine'?"

"As long as ye hold yer pate high an' steal what ye can from the salver."

That was the last contact I had with the Conklin. The next day I was on a bus for Dublin. Three days after that I was wearing a haircut, a new suit, wingtip shoes, and a leather briefcase. Armed with glossy five-by-sevens of the *fomor* Dryr, I daily made my way to the business heart of Dublin and strode through the massive revolving door of a twenty-nine-story glass and steel tower on Talbot Street—the headquarters of the Global Progress Group. During business hours, I drank endless cups of tea in one or another of the six posh restaurants or explored the building. I would ride one or another of the twelve high-speed elevators to explore each floor, hoping to spot Winfield Farrell or Dierdre Hynes. After a few days, my face had become familiar enough that people began to greet me as if I were a colleague. I had to be careful to avoid conversations, lest I get inquiries about my purpose there.

I e-mailed my department chairman and told him I was doing research and would teach my fall classes in the spring. In the evenings I sat hunched over my computer in my cheap hotel room, studying the history and operations of the bank and its charitable arm, Global Progress Foundation. I searched the news archives and Dublin public records for items on Farrell and Hynes. Interestingly, they both owned condos in the same upscale building, as did several other Global Progress Group directors. I forgot all about sending prayers to the *fomors,* as I had promised the Conklin.

It was around one p.m. on the twelfth of October that I entered the restaurant that shared the twentieth floor with the Global Progress Bank and saw Ms. Hynes at a table with a younger woman and two successful-looking men. I guessed that the men were colleagues of hers, and that the girl was an aide. The restaurant was not crowded. I took a table across the room and ordered crab bisque. I took one of my photos of Dryr from my briefcase, and wrote on the back of it, "I bring you greetings and a recommendation from Dryr, at the *sidh* of Cuimhne." This, I told myself, was a worthy opening gambit. If she showed the least consternation while looking at the photo would tell me whether or not she was indeed a *fomor.* I had planned to sign it "Robert Ar-thine," but on an impulse I signed my real name, Morse Brulay. For good measure I added my e-mail address (with its impressive .edu), and my cell phone number. They would doubtless investigate me if they were going to deal with me. I slipped the photo into a manila envelope, wrote Ms. Hynes' name on it, and gave it to the waiter. "Please deliver this to the lady at…"

"I know Ms. Hynes," he said. "May I ask what this is about?"

"Greetings from a friend of hers," I said. "You may look at it if you like." As he handed her the envelope he gestured toward me, and I bowed. She cast an icy look in my direction, then slowly took the photo from the envelope. I should have anticipated my panic at this moment, but somehow I had excluded real emotion from my fantasy version of it. I had been seeing it through romantic eyes, only as the kind of mythic quest one hears about in the sagas. Watching Ms. Hynes' action at this moment, her opening of my message, drove home with a rush of panic the horror of what I was doing—exposing myself and my plan to a member of this unimaginably powerful and malevolent society. Who the hell did I think I was, to dilly-dally with the *fomors?* I was almost pissing in my pants. When she showed not a hint of puzzlement, I wanted to grab the photo back from her and run. Instead, I sat feeling my heart pound as she slipped it into her purse and turned back to her luncheon conversation without giving me a second look.

The next three days were agony. My phone didn't ring, there were only the usual e-mails. I couldn't think about anything else and wandered the streets of Dublin aimlessly, torn between praying that she would contact me, and hoping to hell that she would not; between planning my next strategic step forward, and fleeing to the Shannon Airport with a ticket home. When my cell phone finally rang, on October 15, I was sitting in a bar, drinking a Guinness and half-watching the television. It was a dreadful British game show in which the audience was asked to rate the nastiness of insults that the contestants aimed at each other. My hand shook so hard I could barely operate my iPhone. "Would you be able to meet Ms. Dierdre Hynes at her home office, McCulloch Road and Deems Street, on Monday next?" said an efficient female voice. Holy shit. What will I do for the next four days? I couldn't go back to Headford, that was over. I longed to have friends in Ireland, but there was no one. As I walked back to my hotel I passed a travel agency and decided to book a weekend trip to London. Anything to divert the mind.

London, it turned out, was a stroke of genius. I went to a taxidermy demonstration; I discovered Ghanian and Azerbaijani cuisine; I listened to deafening rock music and danced at a rave club. My partner for a while that night was an androgynous being whose black-circled eyes stared at nothing from under a shock of spiky purple hair. By two p.m. on Monday, when I rang the bell labeled "Hynes" at McCulloch Road and Deems Street in Dublin, I had managed to put things in a kind of perspective. I was feeling viscerally the extreme danger of my game; but I had explored a slice of the world's surprising and amusing possibilities and confronted the question at every turn: what was the value of a life that risked nothing?

There was a doorman in green and gold livery and a peaked cap. He read my credentials, spoke briefly on his cell phone, then waved me in. "Seventh floor." The seventh was the top floor. The elevator opened directly into a highly exotic atrium. Under a glass ceiling, wild parakeets flew here and there among rainforest ferns, palms, and flowering lianas graced with epiphytes and orchids. Rare carp swam in a small pool fed by a tiny waterfall. The whole thing was pervaded by the sound of distant pan pipes and the sweet-sour smell of jungle. I felt out of place in my suit and tie, and the feeling increased when a door opened and Dierdre Hynes asked me to come in. She looked as though she had been working out at the ballet barre; barefoot, wearing only a pale lavender sleeveless leotard, with a red and gold silk scarf carelessly thrown over her shoulders. Her skin was an even ivory, the lines of her body those of a twenty-year-old. Her thick red hair was held by silver combs in an upswept tousle. I wondered if she greeted everyone this way.

The room I entered carried the theme of the atrium in the direction of elegance. Well-made rattan and wicker furniture with leather cushions; museum-quality objets d' art from Africa, Oceania, the ancient Americas; rare animal skins, and smaller plants.

"Love of the natural, the wild," was all I could think of to say.

"And water, don't forget water," she said, lifting two full wineglasses from a side table and handing me one. Her voice was young, too. "To our friend Dryr," she raised her glass. "How did you happen to meet him?"

I took a deep breath and squared my shoulders. I had prepared by trying to fortify my mind against seduction, but I could already see that my life experience hadn't given me much to work with. "You probably know who I am by now," I said, "and I know who you are, too; at least

I know your origins and something of your customs and your aims. I know that I put myself in great danger by revealing my purpose to you, and I risk it because what I'm searching for is more valuable to me than my life."

"And what is that?" Her tone was casual, light, as if we were discussing the latest movies.

"I'll tell you, but first I beg you to listen to my proposal, to what I offer you and all the *fomors* in return for your favor." She sat on a sofa and leaned back, brushing a stray curl from her forehead, waiting. "The *fomors* are known and respected in your new identities because of the power you still wield over humankind, but it is a sad fame, compared to your earlier glory. Your ancient names and deeds, not to mention your likes and dislikes, are largely forgotten. I offer a way—a new way—for you and your colleagues at the GPB to bring back a good measure of your old brightness, and to keep it for generations." I began to talk about the possibilities of the Deep Code, its use in therapy, in the study of memory. "With my credentials, and the power of the *domhain comharthai,* I can establish an institute, the Global Progress Foundation Institute, for the study of memory. The institute will be a tremendous success. Your names will appear everywhere, at great conferences, in the press, in the halls of learning, the notebooks of students," I went on, "along with the rights and privileges of great benefactors, throughout the human world. You will be the new Carnegies, Rockefellers, McArthurs, Kennedys..."

"You are a Druid, Professor Brulay," she said. "Your art is to mediate between us *fomors* and your mortal kin; but it's never been for our sake that Druids do it. To give you something as valuable as the *domhain comharthai* would be a terrible risk. Why should we trust you? If you released our secrets to the mortal world, that would ruin us, wouldn't it?"

"That would ruin me as well, don't you see? No Druid teaches his magic in the public square. I could exercise the power case by case, keeping the process secret; Global Progress Group could keep the right to sign off on every individual use."

"Then why would we need you at all? We could do this ourselves."

"Why did you need the Druids to begin with? You know why.

Mortals have a terrible fear of anything they don't understand. Druidism used to be an integral part of every human community, something people felt sure of; when it was driven underground the fate of the *fomors* followed suit. I'm a professor of psychology, Ms. Hynes. I don't have to tell you that in the public mind people of my profession are scientists, and that scientists are widely accepted as the Druids of our time."

She regarded me for a moment over the rim of her wineglass. "You intrigue me. Of course I can't give you any answers just like that. I *might* talk to the board, but I'd have to know you better first."

"What is it about my proposal so far that you don't like?"

"Oh, I like it so far," she smiled, "But I love being persuaded. Anyway, you don't need the *domhain comharthai* for your project. The Global Progress Foundation could give you grants, enough to make you the envy of your peers. All you'd have to do is feed us the questions, and we'd feed you the answers. Think about *that.* Your own institute, staff, budget. The Brulay Progress Institute."

I shrugged. "There are hundreds of psychological institutes. Anyway success is not what I want. Think of what I could do for *you.* Conference halls full of eminent men and women hanging on your every word; your logo and your slogan, even your picture, in books and TV documentaries throughout the educated world, familiar as the name of Freud or Kinsey."

"And what you want is the *domhain comharthai."* I could see a certain excitement beginning to build in her eyes. Her face was now animated, her gestures erotic. "I've been looking for a man with ideas. I like you. How much do you make now?"

"Eight thousand a month."

"I could double it. We can keep the Deep Code issue open."

"That's very kind of you. I'm flattered, really."

"But no?"

"I have a career. I need the Deep Code. You need me to have it."

She was quiet, and I began to feel a pulse of desire in the room. She stood and walked to the window, her step halfway between a prance and a pavane, the way only an aroused woman moves. She turned and approached until we were almost touching, her eyes lowered, waiting.

I could smell her hair. My heart was pounding. "When can I have an answer, then?" I asked.

She backed away a step, her face still enigmatic, teasing. "Don't be an idiot," she said. "Do you think you'll get another chance?"

"If anything could distract me, it would be you, but let's talk about my offer. Will you let me bring it to the board?"

Another pause. The spell was broken. "You'll get word," she said.

"Wonderful, thank you. When can I expect to hear?"

Without answering, she went to a nearby table and picked up an envelope. I saw that it was the one I had delivered to her, with the photo of Dryr. She held it out to me. "You know the names of the board members," she said. "What more does a Druid need to know?" and she winked archly, took me by the arm, and walked me to the door.

Outside, I felt exhausted and confused. Had my hubris put me in even deeper danger? Had the door been slammed, or left slightly ajar? If the latter, what was I supposed to do? Offer prayers and sacrifices to the board members? In what form would the answer come, and how would I recognize it? I staggered back to my hotel room, collapsed into bed, and had a bizarre dream.

I am standing, naked but painted blue, in the courtyard of a small, crude castle, a place teeming with life. Oxen, horses, and geese wander about. People in coarse clothes with odd-looking hats or shawls over their heads walk here and there carrying bundles. They speak a language I don't recognize, but somehow I understand what I hear—everyday chatter about work, friends, toothaches, food. The people around me pay me no attention in spite of my nakedness. I feel completely disoriented and close to panic.

Bit by bit my panic lets up and I decide to explore my surroundings, cautiously. As I walk around the castle I begin to come across well-dressed people who smile and show me things to admire. A middle-aged man dressed in leather, with a gray fur cape and hat, holds up a sword with a magnificently jeweled hilt. I greet him by his name, Llwyd. He holds out his hand and asks me my name. "Esrom," I lie, and squat close to the ground, clasping my hands in a gesture of prayer. Llwyd nods and disappears. A blond boy of about twelve, dressed in blue satin, shows me a bird with iridescent feathers that sings fantastically. I thank him, calling him Taliesin, and he smiles and holds the bird out to me, but again I make the prayer gesture and retreat into the crowd. Dierdre Hynes, in a yellow dress finely embroidered with rings of flies around the sleeves and collar, approaches me, making outrageous eyes. Again I bow, naming her Etain. I blow her a kiss and hurry off. Now I see Dryr, holding a large book, its leather cover embossed in gold and sealed with a golden lock. Our eyes meet. He turns and walks away, but I follow him until he enters a small room at the foot of a turret, where there is a table and chairs. He lays the book on the table and gestures for me to sit down. I remain standing. "Will you open it?" I ask. In response he produces a tiny gold key from his pocket and holds it out to me.

For a moment I stand there, afraid to touch the key. Then I remember that my left hand is painted with the protecting woad and, trembling, I reach that hand out and take the key. I turn it in the lock and open the book. As I look at the hand-lettered vellum pages, it is as if all my experience, in fact all possible experience is instantly burned on a DVD in my mind, and I can effortlessly access any event, anywhere, at any past or future time just by wishing to. In the pages of the book, I see a tableau of the thing I am doing at that moment: I see myself closing the book and handing the key back to Dryr, at which point the state of complete knowledge vanishes altogether. I no sooner see this in the book than the thing itself happens in the dream.

I awoke in a sweat, my heart throbbing with the most agonizing sense of grief and loss. Death, if it deprives us of all consciousness, would be a much more enjoyable experience. This was pure pain, the most intense horror. I had held an unimaginable power in my hands and let it slip away.

Chapter Four

The Echo

I doubted that the manager of my hotel would be pleased to have me making burnt offerings to the *fomors* in my room, even if I only used herbs and pork fat as the Conklin did. Nor was I eager to test the reaction of the Dublin police by trying it in the public parks. I decided to wait a few days on the slim hope that I might actually get a phone call from the directors of Global Progress Group. A week passed. I had an office phone number for Dierdre Hynes, and I left a message there and sent her an e-mail as well. Three more days passed; and by this time I decided there was little point in remaining in Ireland. They had my contact information, I could come back if necessary.

On the flight back to San Francisco I read the notes from my Celtic adventure. Even if I never heard from the *fomors,* I wouldn't call it a total failure. I had gotten to know a real Druid pretty well, and had learned quite a lot about the lore and ritual. I had not disappeared, as mortals in the old tales were said to do, into a dark *sidh,* never to be seen again. (If I had, I thought gloomily, it was unlikely anyone would have come looking for me.) I wrote my daughter, Thelly, a three-page e-mail, touching on the highlights, concluding that we would probably have to look for another approach to the mastery of time travel.

Unfortunately, I was wrong.

Everything went normally my first couple of months home. I completed a draft of an article on the psychology of modern Druidism (in which I didn't even mention *domhain comharthai),* and I worked the material from my experience into two lectures for my shamanism class. The large and small obsessions of my regular life re-asserted themselves. I nagged my two deadbeat graduate students to pass their exams and finish their theses. I pretended to pay attention at dull faculty meetings. I flirted madly and sadly with Celine Trellis, our departmental administrator, who everybody knew was having a relationship with the chairman, Bob Heniston. Thelly was threatening to drop out of school (again) and become a shaman. My sister Ysabel had re-started her rant that our family was a thicket of "bad neurochemical genes" and we all should all be in psychiatric treatment. Maybe she was right, who knows? Like I said, normal life.

In early December, Chairman Heniston e-mailed me to accompany him to a public meeting downtown, on the subject of local zoning codes. I knew he was on the faculty committee on town-and-gown relations, and I knew what to expect at the meeting. The university has its dark side like any other giant organization. Luckily for the surrounding communities, its administrators lack the magic powers of the *fomors,* though their budgets, their arrogance, and their cunning make them dangerous enough. Among the university's antisocial impulses is an insatiable hunger for public resources of all kinds, especially land. In the case at hand, the fuse had been lit when the chancellor decided to turn a nearby block of low-income housing into the site of a new science building. Heniston was no fool. He had guessed that I might feel a tiny bit guilty about having just skipped out of town for the fall semester. I was ripe for an unpleasant assignment—being tapped to bolster his presence at the meeting.

I was irritated but couldn't say no. A phalanx of bookish scientists, who all but flaunted a complete lack of knowledge and interest in local politics, would face a phalanx of angry neighbors. For their part, the neighbors saw the university as a country club of pampered bullies. Caught between them would be a clutch of harassed local officials trying to avoid a brawl, and a pod of jaded journalists hoping to see one. I was well aware that Heniston expected me to add weight to the university's arguments, maybe even scoring a point or two for his department's prestige. The whole thing struck me as an unamusing ritual drama. It resembled a Western movie in which a gang of cowboys strolls into a saloon full of farmers, while the helpless bartenders look on. I planned to duck under the nearest table when the chairs started flying, and stay there until it was over.

At the same time, I felt a certain shame at my own arrogance. This meeting was also an exemplary exercise in the democratic rights I truly believed in. It was something decent people took seriously.

Things started out along the predictable lines. The locals leveled charge after charge—that our faculty felt nothing for community life; that our students' main contribution was to drive up rents and police costs; that local families were not welcome on campus; that campus events produced nothing but traffic jams and litter, and so on. The faculty answered with clearly impatient condescension, reminding us all about the "basic purpose of higher education," the "value to society of scientific research," the "complexity of the situation," and the "high moral standards of academia." The meeting was disorderly. Groans and boos began to greet faculty comments; community speakers evoked a cacophony of encouraging shouts from the audience of neighbors. After an hour of this, something very odd began to happen; my temper began to heat up along with all the others; and as it did so, the residents who spoke began to look and sound to me like clones of one another. They ceased to be shopkeepers and working moms and baseball fans, and became a tribe, a mindless herd, slavishly following a group of leaders whose only goal was to propagate hatred of the educated class.

One of these leaders was an overgrown cassava of a woman who interrupted every opponent with shouts of "Excuse me! Excuse me!" and whose contribution consisted mainly of reciting her one credential: twenty-seven years in the neighborhood. Someone from the Biology Department suggested that the residents send a representative to speak to the Academic Senate, "So that we can hear the community's concerns in a quieter atmosphere."

"Come to you with our hats in our hands, you mean?" shouted Cassava Woman. "Your quiet atmosphere won't change the fact that the University has never been, and never will be, accountable to the people of this town. As citizens, we have the RIGHT to demand that our city government—our CITY GOVERNMENT—make them accountable, and that's what we're going to do!" She turned to her supporters. "Aren't we? Aren't we?" A hailstorm of cheers dissolved into a chant, "SAVE OUR HOMES! SAVE OUR HOMES!"

Tongue-tied, the faculty sat in quiet fury. This was not their milieu. But to my amazement, I found myself standing at the microphone. The moderator banged his gavel for a full minute before the noise subsided enough that I could speak. "The purpose of this meeting was to exchange information, to share views about the project, but no dialogue can take place when people come here already convinced that we, the faculty, are deaf and blind. You're creating that exact situation with your attitude. Well, this deaf blind man is going back to his office. He has work to do. Good luck with your placards and bullhorns." I picked up my briefcase and strode out, and before I reached the door, I saw that at least a half dozen of my colleagues were following suit. Heniston too, passed me in the hallway and clapped me on the shoulder. "I think you spoke for just about all of us, Brulay!" and he hurried off.

It was now dark, a windy fog swirling around the streetlights. The way to my office led through a grove of ancient eucalyptus, and as I entered it I could hear the creaking and groaning of the treetops in the wind.

Suddenly I find myself in a completely distinct reality; not a dream, an actual waking experience, with all my senses in full play. The situation feels completely familiar. I know the place and the people and the situation intimately. I am standing with Lucien, my blood brother in the clan of Drefill, on the narrow pebble beach of a great wide bay called Hoydis on a cold early dawn. We're barefoot, wearing rough handwoven brown tunics, carrying heavy fish nets on our shoulders. We also carry a wooden bucket of fresh water and goatskin bags holding small fish, net-mending tools, and a few sheaves of barley. In front of us on the water's edge is a row of small fishing boats—plain, well-made boats, each of whose wooden prow projects upward in an arc to end in a carved eagle head that looks down at the water when the boat is afloat. These are the boats of our clan, since the beginning of time the only boats permitted to take nets out into Hoydis Bay. Along the beach are rows of fish-drying racks, structures of slender poles about the length of a small mast, tied with leather thongs.

Lucien and I stand for a moment looking out through the thin morning mist into the bay, at another boat, a large, clumsy boat meant for carrying passengers and goods from the far shore to Leath, the half-moon fair a mile or two up the shore. But the boat is not carrying passengers or goods. With our keen fishermen's eyes we can make out men pulling in nets over her side. We know who the boat belongs to, we see it often on the beach in Leath when we sell our fish there. It brings the people called Thergoes, who trade oats, pigs, leather, and ale at the fair. They talk in a singsong voice and smell peculiar but trade honestly. I sometimes play dice with the Thergoe boy called Bress. It was his sister who danced with me on St. Boniface Eve. I haven't seen her since then, to give her the set of bone buttons I carved, hoping I could lift her skirt next time. The thought of her now conceives a bulge in my tunic.

I know why I haven't seen the girl, and why the Thergoe boat is fishing out here just now. Prince Rupero of their land across the bay burned the abbey of his enemies in a fight two years ago; and this summer God sent a terrible storm up Hoydis that destroyed almost all the crops of the Thergoes. They've been trying to trade what little they have left—iron pots and spoons, charcoal, things they carve in wood—but few want these things. Out of mercy we've given them a lot of fish.

Lucien and I drop the nets into our boat and kneel, placing the barley sheaves on the small altar at the foot of the mast. We've just finished our prayers to the saints and to Dovius, our clan ancestor, and have begun the song to Mother Hoydis, when we spy several of our brother Drefill clansmen descending to the beach from the birch wood above, carrying their nets and gear. Their looks are black, and they scarcely bother to greet us.

Mennian, the oldest among our clan, speaks: "They came last St. Delphine's and promised to repay the elders with grain for the right to fish," he growls. "Of course they were given ample dried cod and sent back with a boot to their butts."

"Sure, their stink would drive the fish far out to sea," someone says, and we all laugh.

"You laugh?" bellows Mennian. "Keep laughing when your nets come up empty and the wind drives your boats onto the Rocks of Clops. God and Dovius will punish all of us for this sacrilege of the dirt-fishers' net-casting in Hoydis. They couldn't possibly even know how to pray."

"Aren't they Christians, though?" someone says.

"Thou shalt not steal!" Mennian sneers.

"When they fail to catch anything, maybe they'll just leave," Lucien says.

"We can't leave it to them, the thieving bastards, or they'll come back whenever they want. Take down those fish racks and bring the poles; but slowly, don't let them see what you're doing."

There's muttering. No one moves.

"What!? By the Holy Word! Are you Drefills, who've kept this water sacred and safe since time began? Shall I tell your women that you've traded your dicks for a thumping by pig-fuckers?"

The married men turn to the drying racks and are soon followed by the younger ones. Mennian is pacing among them shouting orders. "Hide the poles in the boats, like this. Don't bring those nets, leave them on the beach!" We push our boats from the beach and climb in. "When we reach them, show the poles," Mennian shouts. "Tell them what you think about them fishing in Hoydis."

There are seven men on the Thergoe boat. They stop their work and wave as we approach, Mennian's boat in the lead. We drop our sails, Mennian throws a rope to their boat, and they pull him in. Each of our six boats does the same, so that the intruders are surrounded. I recognize the faces of a couple of the Thergoes, from the fair.

"You know Hoydis is Drefill waters," Mennian says.

"We know," one of the men says. "Forgive us, the Drefills have been kind to us, but we're in a terrible situation. Our families are hungry." The men in our boats begin to pull the drying poles out and stand them on end. "Of course you have your rights," says another of the Thergoes, "and we've always respected them. Our

people are at peace. Raspar from your village married our cousin Claris in the time of my father. We only ask for a short while. There are a lot of fish in Hoydis."

"There are a lot of fish in the open sea," says Mennian. "These you've stolen from our water, throw them back!" The word "stolen" fixes everyone like a thunderclap. The only sound is the scraping and thudding of our gunwales against theirs. Everyone is breathing heavily, our breath steaming in the morning cold. Then with a great scream, one of our men lunges with his pole at the Thergoe leader. The man grabs the pole but falls among the nets and fish and water, and suddenly everyone is shouting, poles are swinging, men are climbing into the Thergoe boat, fists are flying. One of the injured Thergoes is thrown overboard and begins to scream horribly, thrashing in the icy water. Another tries to throw him a rope but is cut down with the end of a pole. Someone grabs my throat from behind with a grip of iron, but before I pass out Lucien appears and sinks his teeth into one of the choking hands. One by one our men throw the enemy's own nets over them, then kick and pummel them until they fall. Blood is everywhere. The screaming is unbearable.

"Throw these fish and nets overboard," shouts Mennian.

When we've done so, we climb back into our own boats and make for shore, passing as we do the corpse of the drowned Thergoe, his brown hair splayed out on the water, his head bobbing as though he were conversing with the fish below. My neck aches horribly, my hands are swollen and blue; the left side of Lucien's face is a suppurating red sore, his left eye swollen shut, but the tears in our eyes are pure joy. One of our men begins an old Drefill hymn, and we lustily join in until our voices echo from the rocks above Hoydis.

Dizziness, nausea. I was suddenly back in the eucalyptus grove, holding onto the back of a bench, shaking, terrified. I felt my neck, I looked at my hands. Normal. I sat down, breathing hard, wrestling for control. After a few minutes I began to calm down enough to think about the experience, turn it over in my mind. The people around me in the flashback were Caucasians, so I guessed the continent must have been Europe. What part of Europe? The language we were speaking had sounded like a Romance language but not a modern one. It could have been an earlier version of French, or Portuguese, I thought. Knowing little of European history, I guessed from the technology that it was pre-Renaissance; maybe early Middle Ages. But what had I been doing there? Visiting some previous life? Connecting with an ancestral memory?

Then it dawned on me. Yes. There could be no doubt. The whole shocking thing, the flashback, was a direct result of my search for the Deep Code, but how or why I could only guess. I had certainly not willed this, and I certainly had no control over it. The thought that it might happen again was horrifying. Was this what the Conklin had meant, when he warned me about a curse following my mistake at the *sidh* of Cuimhne? Was I doomed from this day forward to be caught at any moment by a nightmarish flashback? I buried my face in my hands and began to cry.

Over the next few weeks I was clearly suffering from a mild case of post-traumatic stress. Thoughts of the Deep Code flashback would force themselves into my mind at odd moments, and I found myself unable to concentrate. I felt depressed. A face, or a smell, would remind me of it, and I would startle, my heart suddenly pounding. I found I couldn't pass a fish market or even go near the shore of San Francisco Bay without an upsurge of irrational fear. The sight of sailboats, or even paintings of them, depressed me.

But gradually the terrible vividness of it began to fade; it began to feel more like an exceptionally strong nightmare. I found myself beginning to explore, tentatively at first, questions about its meaning. First, there was the question of its emotional impact. Because it had none of the characteristics of a dream or a hallucination, I had to accept either that it had "really happened," that it was literally a form of vivid memory, or that it represented a form of profound insanity, an inability to distinguish internal from external events. I began to understand why even intelligent schizophrenics prefer to believe in the independent reality of their hallucinations. But to accept it as real meant that I had to accept it as an incident in my actual ancestral past—in some ways a worse proposition than the notion that I was insane. I had participated in a murder. I had brutalized fellow human beings who were asking for my kindness, and in a cowardly way at that. I began to ask myself whether I actually did have such feelings and impulses in me, whether my view of myself as a generous, peace-loving, rational person was just an illusion.

Then there was the question of why this *particular* Deep Code experience. Of all the possible "memories" I could have been shown, or shown myself, why this ghastly choice? It was tempting to think about the obvious parallels between the flashback and the meeting I had just left that night. Hadn't I been in the midst of a kind of tribal combat, between my colleagues and our nonacademic neighbors, a conflict involving territory and privilege? Hadn't I stereotyped the "enemy" as an inferior sort, dismissing their claims to equality? Hadn't I been influenced by the presence of authority, my department chairman, to throw my principles aside and act on herd instinct? It seemed so.

In other words, the flashback seemed to be saying, my self-image as an enlightened, rational person with perfect control over my actions was a fiction. My actions had sprung from ancient, primitive impulses programmed into my brain stem, things over which I had almost no control; and I was no different in this respect from any other human being. These thoughts sickened me.

Chapter Five

The Likes of It

I felt like someone with a crippling disease that could flare up unexpectedly at any time, grateful for each day that passed innocently. I kept quiet about it of course. Enough people already thought of me as a nutcase. Weeks went by. One night I awoke from a nightmarish repeat of the episode, but it was clearly only a dream, and it didn't happen again. The fish war flashback, as I now called it, stayed vivid in my memory, but I began to think it might have been a unique experience, a kind of reminder-of-who's-boss from the *fomors*. More likely, it was something that could be explained naturally, through brain chemistry and physiology. I started to look for similar events in the psychology books. It might actually have been a brief psychotic episode, or a kind of accidental self-hypnosis. If it happened again, I might be able to control it with medication.

And after all, it seemed that I could not have been actually injured by the flashback. The horror of it sprang simply from its intensity, its realism, and my inability to control it. Maybe it was really a creative dream with a positive message: Was the tribal mentality of the fish war flashback something that was affecting my everyday life? If I dwelt on the idea, it seemed to have some value. "You can't park there, that's *my* spot." "How dare the *Dean* try to tell our faculty we can't admit this student?" "*Those* people don't belong in this restaurant—look how they're dressed." Aren't these just tiny examples of the same sort of mentality that had surged to the point of violent madness there on Hoydis Bay?

Suppose I could actually learn to repeat this kind of experience, to induce it in myself, or in others? Might there not be the possibility here of a scientific breakthrough, and insight into human intolerance and violence? Maybe my quest for the Deep Code had not been entirely in vain after all. But I had no idea how to pursue this line of thought, unless I went back to Ireland, and that seemed not only unlikely to succeed, but dangerous as well.

Anyway, life as usual gave me plenty of other things to think about. An article I wrote on the psychology of Druidism was accepted for publication in *Clinical Science International.* By some hiccup of fate the dean of the science faculty heard about it, and through some spasm of judgment he asked me to give the campus-wide Spring Lecture in March. My name went on engraved invitations. My chairman was mystified, as to tell you the truth was I. I was used to giving papers at scientific meetings, sometimes even invited ones, but the audiences at those things were invariably a tiny collection of eccentrics like myself, aficionados of shamanism and the occult, people who understood the background of my work, and who needed no persuasion to take it seriously. This was another matter, a truly rare opportunity to explain my work to people who knew little of such things, in a setting where I would be taken seriously. I wouldn't say I was jubilant. Given the eccentricity of my viewpoint in academia, there was plenty of room for failure. Still, I felt sure of the value of my work, and I knew the general mentality of my audience. At the very least, the choice of my specialty for the Spring Lecture would lend it a crumb of dignity; with a forceful presentation, I might actually win a convert or two among the more open-minded students.

This shouldn't be very difficult, I said to myself.

One might as well invite a cat for a swim as ask our faculty to indulge in gaiety, but the Spring Lecture had more than a hint of festivity to it. Cut flowers were arrayed on tables in the lobby of the main auditorium, the program was printed in lavender on gold paper, the chatter of faculty and students seemed a bit more animated than usual as they settled into their seats, the dean even cracked a joke during the introduction. "We have a number of distinguished guests from our sister institutions of learning here today, and to them I would only like to say that, in showing off the talents of our faculty here, we do not mean to assert our superiority. The commercial world may be dog-eat-dog, but here in academia it's exactly the other way around."

At last, the podium was mine:

> The Druids are chiefly known, in our sensation-hungry century, for having practiced human sacrifice, and I wouldn't be surprised if some of you came here today out of curiosity about that. After all, one rarely hears about such bloodthirsty things, unless of course one studies the Biblical Middle East, the native civilizations of the Americas, classical Greek, Roman, or Hindu cultures, medieval Europe, or precolonial Africa or Oceania. I'm sorry to say I'm not going to talk about human sacrifice; I want instead to focus on the roles of the Druids as the guardians of knowledge, and on how they used symbols to protect and enhance those roles...

I talked about how the Druids studied the movements of the planets and stars, just as the ancients sages in every part of the world had done, giving them not only the power to predict nature, but the illusion of control over it as well. In an era of human thought when every detail of life was attributed to the will of some conscious spirit, all power arose in the knowledge of such supernatural intentions. This knowledge was as precious then—or perhaps more so—as military might or money is today; and it was perfected, guarded, traded, stolen, and destroyed just as our modern sources of power are. Druidic knowledge was encoded in the long sagas they memorized—of Cuchulainn and Meave and Peredur, Taliesin, Élathin, and Danán, and these tales themselves came to embody the power of their heroes. The person who knew the tales also knew the language of the spirits, could speak with them, learn their intentions, persuade them for or against a cause.

Over many centuries, the whole body of Druidic lore was distilled, by a kind of natural selection, retaining such lore as most swayed human minds and hearts, adjusting the bits of intelligence one to the other, until they fit together like the bits of brilliant glass in a giant cathedral window, painting a picture of a coherent, awe-inspiring universe, a universe of which the Druids themselves were the guardians and interpreters.

I ended with the *domhain comharthai,* showing how, as a theory of time, it explained the extraordinary abilities of the Druids. Exactly like Plato's allegory of the cave, in which humans struggle to understand the world by watching mere shadows thrown by fire on a wall, the human view of linear time is shown by the *domhain comharthai* to be a feeble illusion, an illusion from which the agile Druid mind is awakened. In the awakened state, the Druid has access to the whole panoply of time, viewing the world of human cares as a soaring eagle views a plain, a vista in which absolutely nothing is hidden. This was the essence of his authority, just as in our times, authority resides in specialized knowledge of the *de-spiritualized,* mechanical forces that direct human nature and the universe.

The applause was just enough to express the good manners that were standard in that hall. Following the custom of the Spring Lecture, I offered to take questions. What about human sacrifice? someone asked.

"If you believe that the giving of one human life is necessary to sustain many lives, you do it," I said. "In our culture, we have three names for it: war, terrorism, and execution. The Druidic version was probably more humane, because in some of its forms it guaranteed the victim eternal life, and may have been actively sought."

A young man raised his hand in one of the middle rows, and I acknowledged him. When he stood, I recognized him. Doctor Kroker, a junior instructor in my department, a lab psychologist whom Chairman Heniston had recruited in his efforts to make his fiefdom more respectably scientific. Today Kroker was flanked by several of his student lab assistants. "This lecture is supposed to be an example of the best thinking of our science faculty," Kroker said, "and I'm surprised to find no actual science in it at all." He paused until the murmur of surprise faded. "Science is knowledge based on testable evidence, yet you have offered no such thing—nothing, really, other than your own conjecture. I could give a completely different account of the Druidic culture, and none of you could refute it." The murmuring resumed for a moment, then there was silence. Kroker remained standing, waiting for a response.

I stood for a moment dumbfounded by the absurdity of his challenge and infuriated by his lack of manners. I could have given him, then and there, a list of books to read on the history and philosophy of science, where he would find that competing theories often enjoy equal attention until one proves more useful than another. What happened next must have only taken a few seconds—much less time than it will take to read it.

It's dark and the bare ground on which I walk is frozen. I am entering a large hutlike structure of poles and bark, where six other men wait. All of us are dressed in animal skins and carry spears and bows. I am the only one who also wears a heavy mantle of soft fur, the edges of which are decorated with feathers and boar's teeth, and a conch shell hangs on a thong from my belt. Several wolfish dogs whine and yap, prowling in the darkness behind me as I enter. There's a fire in the room, and no one seems to notice the thick smoke from it, nor do we mind the smell of unwashed human bodies. A very old man sits at the back of the room, beating rhythmically on a small drum and singing, a prayer to the guardian spirits of our clan.

"Where are the other men?" I ask. "Raxel, Thurn, Ostus...?"

There's an awkward silence, then someone says, "Raxel said they were going with Engren. He says he knows a better place."

I feel the hair rise on the back of my neck. "And does he?" There is silence. They stare at each other, or at the ground. "Come with me, then!" As I turn and stride into the dark, I can hear the others catching up their gear and following me. We walk up a stony hill about a hundred paces until we come to a row of small huts along the bank of a frozen stream, and hear the murmur of men's voices. Approaching one of the huts I yank aside the skin that serves as a door, and enter. There are two young men, a woman, and a girl child of about four summers in the hut. My comrades assemble at the door, looking in. I address one of the young men in the hut. "Engren, you are leading a separate hunt?"

He stands and eyes me steadily. "I know a better place, Godoc. The knowledge was brought to me by a white owl last night. The owl showed me where he opened a warm spring there, where the reindeer drink."

"Good!" I say. "Take all the men you want." I step outside, raise my conch shell to my lips, and sound a long, clear note. The men crouch in a circle around me, talking softly. The dogs also sit at a distance and wait. Dawn is beginning to lighten the sky to the east. One by one, others come from the surrounding huts and join the circle, until there are about twenty people present. "Engren says he has found a better place to hunt," I say to the crowd. "He claims the white owl as his guardian spirit, as his grandfather did. Those who are really favored by this spirit are lucky; but those who falsely claim its favor always come to a bad end. Anyone who wants may go with Engren. If you do, he and he alone will lead your hunting from now on. Those who prefer to hunt with me, come with me now. We are going." I stride off down the hill without looking back, and I can hear the crunch of many footsteps on the frozen ground. I also hear the sound of Engren's wife wailing uncontrollably, and I know that not a single man has stayed behind. Engren and his family will be gone from here forever before we return from the hunt.

I stood at the lectern, trembling, stunned, and speechless. Seeing my confusion, Dean Ripley stood and addressed the audience. "I believe that's all the time we have for questions, ladies and gentlemen. Thank you for coming, and thanks to Professor Brulay. We have wine and tidbits in the lobby for those of you who would like to stay and mingle." As the crowd began to leave he touched my elbow. "All you all right, Brulay? That was rather ill mannered, I thought…"

"I just had this…kind of a spell, I guess."

"You'd better go on home, then. Don't have to stay if you're not well…"

"No, no. I'll be okay."

As my normal state returned, I realized dimly that I had performed like a complete idiot, but my mind was absorbed by another, far blacker thought: The fish war flashback had not been an anomaly, but the symptom of a chronic condition. When would the next episode strike? How could I prepare myself for it? On one hand I wanted to flee, to hide my face from this complacent crowd and nurse my wounded pride, and on the other hand I feared being alone. The handshakes and vague pleasantries were reassuring, I really was myself, here, and not some lost ghost, caught in the wilderness of the *domhain comharthai*. Thankfully, neither Kroker nor Chairman Heniston was there in the lobby to remind me of what had happened in the auditorium.

When the crowd finally drifted away I was still afraid of being alone. I drove to a pleasant lounge downtown and sat at the bar, sipping several margaritas while I replayed the scene over and over. At length time and the alcohol calmed me, and I began to wonder what message, what significance, I could dredge from the experience this time. Again, there had been a clear overlap between the trigger experience and the flashback, and this time it had to do with symbolism and authority. In my mind I replaced the disastrous outcome of the afternoon:

"Excuse me, Dean Ripley," I might have said as he stood to announce the end of the lecture. "I'd just like to respond to Dr. Kroker's very interesting question. Can everyone please sit down for a second? Just for a moment. There, thanks. Ladies and gentlemen, what we're witnessing right now, here in this auditorium, is a fascinating and possibly enlightening human situation, a primordial drama of the sort that unconsciously shapes all of our lives and often determines our destinies." I now have people's attention again, and the hubbub settles down. "In our own culture, as among the Druids, symbols of power, and the authority based on them, often determine the course of events for better or for worse. But power is always in short supply, it is always contested by those who want more. Today, I, Morse Brulay, stand before you draped in the powerful symbolism of the Spring Lecture, an icon of our culture's homage to scientific knowledge, and those who guard and produce it. Is this not the equivalent of homage to the spirits of Celtic mythology, and the skill of the Druids as mediators between myth and everyday life? In

a classic move far older than Druidism, Dr. Kroker has chosen to challenge my authority, claiming that his knowledge is truer than mine. Claiming, if you will, that he is the one, not I, who truly speaks the language of that great god, Science. Is he correct? How are we to know? He wields the mighty symbol of the laboratory; and yet he's young and has yet to distinguish himself among his fellow Druids. He and I could stand here and trade magic formulae, trade symbols of power, and we would simply be re-enacting a human drama that hasn't essentially changed in fifty millennia, and will not change in the next fifty, if our species lives that long. And so I say, Bravo, Dr. Kroker, keep brandishing those symbols, and thanks for the illustration of my talk." I collect my notes, bow, and step down from the podium. There is little applause, and I surmise that although I had failed to make myself clear to most of the audience, perhaps a few perceptive souls had caught my point.

As I finished my third margarita, I could almost hear the *fomors* laughing in their *sidhs.*

Chapter Six

Sex Lesson

About a week after the Spring Lecture fiasco another very strange thing happened. I was keeping a low profile in the department. It wasn't difficult to avoid meeting my colleagues if I just stayed away from unnecessary meetings and seminars and stuck to my teaching. In order to protect time for their research, most faculty spent a good deal of time working at home, or huddled behind locked office doors. Students with urgent requests usually had to waylay their advisors outside their classrooms. For once I was grateful for the way voice mail and e-mail had turned human social life into the valley of the hermits.

There was a semiannual meeting of the department's Committee on Research Space, which I couldn't avoid because I chaired it. It was my job to keep track of who was doing what, where, and with whom. The job didn't improve one's popularity. Overworked office staff disliked chasing faculty around getting answers to these questions; the faculty themselves disliked being asked. Some didn't want their colleagues knowing they were doing very little, with very few. Others resented attention to the fact that they had usurped others' space to build their empires.

Reports and requests from the committee went to Chairman Bob Heniston, and all final decisions were his, but Celine Trellis, his able administrator, was the one who actually knew what was going on, who actually ran the place. If you wanted anything at all done, she was the one, and it behooved the rest of us to study her priorities and foibles carefully. Everyone knew that she and Heniston had, shall we say, more than a professional relationship in spite of his married state, and of course this was strictly a no-fly zone around the office. The morally fastidious facade of the university conceals a buzzing hive of passions, like any other giant human enterprise. People who mistake the written rules for the operative system have extremely short careers.

As I mentioned earlier, I found Celine Trellis exciting, and I don't think she disliked me, but our relationship stood on somewhat soggy ground. I was a senior professor and had to be treated politely, but I often had to ask her for favors that weren't easy to provide. Prying information out of surly faculty is a perfect example. Then there was her closeness to Bob Heniston. The chairman found my grumpy eccentricity galling, and I think he would have fired me if I hadn't had the protection of tenure. I in turn disrespected his cautious conventionality, his lack of imagination. How was I to know what tidbits involving me might pass between Celine and him in moments of intimacy?

The words "courteous" and "efficient," then, would pretty much describe my relationship with her. I knew almost nothing about her personality or private life (aside from the unmentionable fact I just mentioned), and I supposed vice versa. I tried to avoid asking for favors if I could do the work myself. If I did need something, I'd ask her whether she was busy. I tried to anticipate needs in advance so that I needn't ask her to rush. I made a point of thanking her and complimenting her on her skills. If she asked for something from me, I did my best to do it quickly and well, and she gave me the same courtesy.

And so it was that when three members of the faculty presented requests for additional space at the space committee meeting, it fell to me to ask Celine for a new general assessment of faculty assignments and needs. I knew she preferred that such things be submitted in memo form, but I always delivered my memos to her office in person and chatted with her about them. This time, while we were going over the basics of my memo, I noticed that her usually focused gaze was wandering, her usually crisp answers a bit vague, and her usually probing questions missing altogether.

"I can see you have something major on your mind," I finally said in as sympathetic a voice as I could muster. "Is it something I can help with?"

She sat looking at me for a minute, pensive, unsure. "It's typical of you to ask."

"It is?"

"Yeah. You think about people. I noticed the way you treated Dr. Kroker at the Spring Lecture. You could have called him on his childish question, but you didn't want to embarrass him."

"Uh, thanks. I just couldn't think of a clever comeback right then. His question was a complex one and deserved a complex answer."

"See? Most people would have just told him, in effect, to stick it."

"You give me too much credit."

"No. You never talk down to people. I wish…" She looked down and fidgeted with a pad of post-its.

"Wish what?"

She sighed heavily. "Nothing."

"I'm open to talk any time. Just let me know."

Regaining her composure, she nodded briskly, brandished my memo, said thanks, she'd get right on it, and turned to her computer screen.

As I walked back to my office I felt like someone who's just discovered the entrance to a hidden corridor in his basement. Here was a very large and very mysterious chunk of information I had never suspected was there. It was shocking enough to discover that Celine Trellis had an opinion—a very flattering opinion—about my character. She had apparently formed this opinion through careful observation. This opinion was something that might, or might not, completely change our relationship.

What was it that I'd missed about her? As I searched my memory I began to put together bits of disregarded fact. She often collected things for charity—clothes for the victims of Hurricane Katrina, money for the Myanmar protestors; she sent out flowery memos whenever anyone in the department (especially the chairman) won an honor; she had a poster from the Wizard of Oz in her office, she remembered the secretaries' birthdays. Celine Trellis was the one person who day after day commanded the respect of our adolescent faculty, frightened

Admin's lazy bureaucrats into doing their jobs, deflected the hostile ambitions of our sister departments. She worked late at her desk three nights out of five.

And lo, she was a hopeless romantic.

But what really blew my mind was that she wanted me to know it, to take it into account. It was almost like one of the flashbacks; with a single short conversation, she had bounced me to a place where I could never look at her in anything like the same way again.

When you're forced by circumstances to radically change your way of looking at things, you find yourself entertaining all kinds of odd ideas that you would have brushed off normally. One of the lessons of my flashbacks was that our linear sense of time really is an illusion. If you dwell on that, you start to wonder what it might reveal about the so-called future. Is it all prefigured in the past, and is the idea that we can influence it just another illusion? Are we surrounded by signs that we might learn to read, laying the future open to us? Are the seemingly random events of our lives really threads in a tightly woven tapestry, whose pattern would become clear if we could only stand back from it? Is this the shared secret of the seers of history, from Cassandra to Nostradamus? It seemed crazy to think so, and yet I had to find out what the message might be of this strange twist in my perception of Celine. I had to find out where it might lead, but it would take the greatest subtlety. That idea made me laugh, too. Who was I hiding from? The *fomors* knew—maybe even programmed—my every move. If Celine were part of a foreordained plan, I shouldn't have to "do" anything at all, right? The trouble was, now I could scarcely think of anything else.

A week later she e-mailed me the data I had asked for, offering to clear up any questions I might have. I wrote back, saying that since she knew the operations and personalities of the department far better than I did, I would like to have her advice about some space decisions.

As I walked down the hall to her office, I could feel my heart pounding and, when I got there, made an effort to appear calm and businesslike. She had on a thin tan cardigan sweater over a cream-colored silk blouse with rows of little pleats. Her long, straight brown hair was held at the temples with plain silver clips. Her eyes, calm and businesslike as usual, looked a bit larger and darker this time. I thought I saw the tiniest fleck of errant mascara at the outer corner of the left one. My heart sank a bit. In her face and voice there was not even a veiled hint of our last exchange. Should I steer the conversation back to it?

"You're looking a bit more, ah, relaxed today," I ventured.

She ignored the lead, turning our attention at once to the question of office space. Shit. I was making too much of this. Shit, shit, shit. Better leave it alone. I went back to my office, glared for a moment at the clutter on my desk and the blinking message light on my phone, grabbed my briefcase, slammed the door as I left, and went home.

It was after dinner that I opened my e-mail and found another message from her.

Morse: There is something I forgot to mention in our meeting today. Will you be in your office tomorrow? —Thanks, Celine

My heart began to pound again. Was this it? I had planned on working at home the next day, but I wrote back that I would be in my office from nine to five, then changed it to say afternoon.

She phoned me at about 1:20 to see if I was in, then came to my office with a sheaf of papers and a hand calculator, looking a little tired and nervous. She showed me a memo from the dean's office outlining new guidelines on departmental space requests. I looked at it and saw that it was almost two years old, and I understood this was not why she was here. I took several deep breaths to calm myself. We spent two minutes discussing the memo, then I said, "There's something else on your mind."

She feigned surprise. "Tsk, tsk, you psychologists."

"Okay." I pushed my swivel chair back and stood up. She stood, went to the door and opened it, hesitated, her head down.

"Have time for a cup of coffee?" I asked. She closed the door and came back but did not sit. A long silence while she gazed out the window over my shoulder.

"I have this boyfriend, he's married."

"I know. Everybody knows, but that's not a problem. They've known for a long time. I guess you want out?"

"They know who it is?"

I nodded.

"I need a strategy."

"Talk to me about it. You know you can trust me, don't you?" I reached over and switched off my desk phone.

"Yes, I know. You're the only one." She sat down. "Bob was tremendously helpful during my divorce two years ago. He listened to me by the hour, he gave me paid days off, he even helped me get legal help. I needed him, and I started to feel that I loved him. He needed me too. His marriage was a mess, he'd already had an affair that had broken his heart." She began to pace the room. "The longer this goes on, the more guilty we feel, and the more we fight. Now he's talking about a divorce. He wants me to take a vacation in Europe with him. But I don't want to. Morse, it would be a huge mistake for him to get divorced. I know it. I have to talk him out of it, and the only way I can is to show him that we don't really love each other enough to carry that around." She stopped and wiped the corner of her eye. My whole body was throbbing.

"This is very scary for you," I said. "Doing the right thing is going to hurt both of you. Hurt a lot. It's a question of whether not doing it will hurt more, but you already know that."

She nodded, looking miserable.

"What about therapy?"

She shook her head. "He'd never do it. He keeps saying that he has insight, that he knows what he's doing, that everything will be all right. But I know it won't." She paused again. "He knows I won't expose him. That's not my style, and besides, if it was just my word against his, the system would protect him. I know, I've seen it."

"You have to have a third person. Who's your support system?"

"I haven't worked on that in a long time, I'm sorry to say. My mom and dad, my sister, they'd stand by me, but they're just not the type for this kind of thing, know what I mean? Neither are my friends. This damn job is my whole life."

"I see. What about me?"

"What? You? Talk to him?" She shook her head vehemently. "It would kill him if he knew I talked to you."

"It wouldn't kill him. Anyway, I could get him to tell me himself. I could meet with the two of you, and we could start from the beginning."

"Excuse me, I know you're trying to…to be helpful, but that's, well, not helpful." She laughed darkly. "You might as well just shoot him. Shoot both of us, while you're at it."

"What if you had someone else—another, um, suitor?"

"Another love interest?" She looked at me hard then and saw what I meant. "No, no, Morse. Jesus. Don't make it more complicated than it is."

"It might turn out to be very simple."

She stood up again. "I've got to get back to work. Thanks so much."

"You're a romantic, Celine. I've studied you. I'm sorry to say, you'll always be in love trouble. You can't live without it. All you can do is follow your heart." As she stepped out the door I said it again, "Follow your heart."

She turned. "Damn! I knew I should've kept my mouth shut!" She closed the door and I heard her quick footsteps in the hall.

In that moment I knew I was a transformed man. I had been here before, on this high plateau of exquisite pain, the place where love first takes hold, the place where you feel your soul stretched out like a great red kite diving and swooping into a sweet and terrible thunderstorm. Did she feel it too? Maybe a little. Her anger was the anger of being tested, of bumping against the boundaries she had set herself, of raging against what she really wanted in some wild inadmissible way. As soon as she was gone I went to my car and drove to the costume store area of Haight Street, where I found an oversized white lab coat, a red and yellow toy stethoscope, a frizzy black wig, and a pair of Groucho Marx glasses attached to the big nose and mustache. I took them back to my office and sat down at my computer. Two hours later I had this sonnet:

Born to love in excess, born to learn
The thrill of fear and hate; born to cry
And laugh, to burn with pride and shame in turn,
Groping for a line between our low and high;
Fearing night, we hide ourselves away
From day, and seek the safety of our caves.
Appetite (the sainted voices say)
And aversion make of us their slaves.
Our myths of paradise say, Cut your heart to size,
Nor grieve the loss of what you amputate,
But seek a twilight sure to minimize
The glare and darkness of your native state.
Ignore such fools as sing a different song.
So sane a life, you know, is far too long.

I printed it in 20-point type and folded it in three. It was now 4:45. I put on the lab coat and stuffed the poem and the other things in the pockets. I went to the entrance to the parking structure where Celine usually left her car and took up an inconspicuous position. Five p.m. came and went. Five-fifteen. Five-thirty. At five forty-seven I was about to give up when I saw her coming across the street. I quickly put the stuff on and showed myself.

"Guten abend! I hear you heff been lookink for ze cure of ze getraumatized ticker! Ich bin Herr Professor Doktor Sigmund Fraud..."

When she recognized my voice she scowled and quickened her step, but I trotted alongside, and her scowl slowly melted into a smile. "Go away!" she giggled. "Gehen sie!"

I held out the poem. "Ich habe here ein magiker geformula, wunderbar for ze ticker!" As she was about to take it, I glanced over her shoulder, and who should I see approaching but Bob Heniston. He was smiling broadly, apparently taking me for an anonymous street performer. "Hi, darling!" he called to her.

She turned quickly to me and said loudly, "Go away, whoever you are! I don't want your magic whatever!" Mutely, I offered the poem to

Bob, but he smiled, shook his head, slipped his arm around her waist, and kissed her on the ear as they walked.

Dust devils move across the plain below my perch on a rocky outcropping on the side of a low hill. In my right hand I hold a clump of acacia pods, which I break open one by one with my teeth. I feel the hot wind stir my fur, already erect like my penis, as subtle whiffs from the body of a young female drift up through the heat. I mounted her just for fun last summer, before she had breasts or the smell that now tells me she is fertile. Farther out on the plain, older females with their young move in a loose group, foraging for seeds and insects. Here below me, the fertile one and two premenstrual females are being kept in view by the big male who has been mounting her from time to time for the past three days. An antelope thighbone beside him, he rests against a fallen log with his eyes almost closed, but I know he is watching me. He has fought off several other males already, and he's probably tired, perhaps injured. The females see me too, and their meandering forage course brings them ever closer to my perch. From time to time the younger ones throw clumps of grass, chase each other, giggle, excited by the situation they know is developing. At last the object of my arousal gets bored and lies down in the grass. She sighs and stretches as one of the juveniles snuggles up to her and begins to masturbate.

My muscles are quivering, I feel the strength of rage rising in my limbs. I pick up a good-sized rock with jagged edges and walk slowly down toward the females. Immediately the big male springs to his feet and attacks, driving the screaming females left and right, then running straight at me. I lift the rock above my head and counterattack from my higher ground, howling, all my fear now turned to fury. My enemy strikes the ground with his bone club, throwing dust in my face, but when I am almost upon him he whirls and retreats. I am faster, and I bring the rock down hard, aiming at his head. He ducks and I miss but open a deep gash on his shoulder. Whirling, he grabs me and lifts me from the ground. I am amazed by his strength. I hear howls from the rest of the troop as we thrash on the ground. I see blood streaming from my arm where he has bitten me, but in my rage I barely feel it. As he begins to tire I get on top of him, grasp the dense fur on his head, and with all my strength grind his face into the hard earth until he goes limp. Panting, I stand, grab his club, and strike his skull repeatedly until I feel it crack. I drop the club and go to take my prize who squats nearby, trembling with excitement.

I came to my senses shaking and dizzy, but my vertigo was still overwhelmed by another feeling: lust. Raging, consuming, maddening lust. Celine and Heniston were nowhere in sight. I ran after them, searching among the cars until I saw them walking ahead of me in the half dark. I caught up. I pulled off my disguise. Heniston, turning pale, greeted me with mock joviality. "Why, It's you, Morse! Ha ha, is this some sort of experiment?"

I ignored him and went down on one knee in front of Celine, panting, and grabbed her hand. "Will you go out with me?" She pulled her hand away and glanced at Henisten, laughing nervously.

"Uhh, that depends..."

"On the conditions? I can tell you the conditions right now. Dinner and a show. You pick the time and place." She looked at Heniston, and the hair stood up on my neck. My right hand itched to punch him in the face. "A double date," I said. "With Bob, here, and Marilyn. That's your wife's name, isn't it, Bob? Marilyn? What do you say?" He froze, feeling my hatred.

"Um, why don't you call me, Morse?" she said.

"Why can't you tell me now? Do you have to clear it with someone?"

"Leave her alone, Brulay," he said.

"You'd like that, wouldn't you? You'd like everyone to leave her alone. But it's not your decision, is it?"

"You're making a fool of yourself," he said.

I looked at Celine. "Is someone here making a fool of himself?"

She sighed. "You've made your point, Morse, now please..."

"My *point?* Just what is my *point?*" Silence. I stood slowly and turned my back on them. My footsteps echoed as I strode off through the darkening lot. In a moment, the evening lights came on throughout the parking structure.

I don't know how I got home, I was still in vertigo, nauseated. I grabbed a bottle of Chardonnay from the refrigerator and drank half of it straight off, cursing the *fomors,* cursing the photos I had taken at the *sidh* of Cuimhne. The phone rang but I didn't answer it and the caller left no message. As my thoughts calmed and slowed to a more normal pace I saw that my entire life was becoming a ludicrous joke. Social standing, collegiality, intellectual achievement, love, they were all pompous self-delusion, greasepaint over the crude savagery of our nature. What was left? Kindness? Humility? Could ascetic self-denial be the flotsam of my life's shipwreck, something to hang onto while everything else sank into a sea of cynicism and despair? If so, did I have the strength embrace it? And even if I did, would it, too, eventually crumble and sink in the toxic waters of the *domhain comharthai?* One thing was becoming clear. I couldn't keep living this way, in this place, with this job, among these people. This life was a disintegrating fabric of false habits and assumptions. There might not be any sounder place, anywhere I went might be just another stage setting, innocent in its unfamiliarity but just as doomed as this one, and I might be hounded from one to the other until death gave me relief. With that thought, exhaustion caught up with me and I slept.

Chapter Seven

Time Out

When I woke the next morning I remembered only the generalities of last evening. In a fit of lust and rage, I had insulted Heniston. Well, somebody had to do it. Anyway, he had always thought of me as an oddball, and besides, I'd had it with this place, this so-called career. Everything about it had ceased to interest me, except maybe Celine, and she had her own fish to fry.

This wouldn't be the first time I had jumped ship, so to speak, abandoning my profession and my home in search of some deeper meaning. A few years ago I thought I had found that meaning, but it slipped away with time. Those years had formed a great circle that had led me across the world, in and out of madness, and back here. But now the sense of things, the reason for living, were definitely slipping away again—or maybe I should say, were been stolen away by the *fomors.* At any rate, I no longer had the fear that most people have of radical change.

The question was, change to what? As I analyzed my painful wakening, I saw it as a deep awareness of something we all sense vaguely but manage to keep hidden away in a dark corner of consciousness: the fantastic hypocrisy of what we are pleased to call civilization. I thought of the great novelist Nagai Kafu. Sickened by the falseness of Tokyo's "proper wives," Kafu found truth and decency in "what was from the start taken to be dark and unrighteous." He had chosen as his milieu the lives of whores and drunkards in the city's gay quarters a hundred years ago.

There are plenty of places like that in the world, but no, what I wanted was not despair so much as simple affirmation of the primitive, the unrefined. The world of the old Druids, perhaps. In paying homage to the *fomors,* weren't they acknowledging their own animal nature, their own violent desires and fears? Was there any place in the modern world with at least this much honesty and insight? Or had even the most primitive places—the Kalahari Desert, the Amazon jungle—been infected by the world monoculture, the nervous amalgam of vanity and self-indulgence that my nightmare flashbacks mocked?

As I sat at my computer and logged on to my e-mail it occurred to me that the main function of our technology is to keep us frozen in this state, congratulating ourselves for the superiority of our intelligence, the watchlike precision of our institutions and instruments, even as it slips layer after layer of distracting trivia between our actions and their meanings.

Today as usual I had dozens of new e-mails. My eye lit instantly on one from Celine. Just looking at her name in the "From" column gave me illusion that I smelled gardenias.

Hi, Morse,
It would seem that we have some rather complex issues to talk over. As far as meeting times, what is your schedule like?
Best, Celine

You're a fool if you respond to this, I said to myself, and an even bigger fool if you don't. I picked up the phone and called her. She took the phone and said she was tied up but would come by my office at five. A half hour later, she called up and canceled, saying she needed time to think.

"Think about what?"

"I'll tell you when I get it sorted out. Morse, I'd like to thank you for what you did yesterday. It was a brilliant strategy. Nothing else would have worked."

"Strategy? What strategy? What worked?"

"Don't tell me you didn't do that on purpose."

"I have no idea what you're talking about."

"Wow. Now I'm *really* confused. I thought your crazy routine was a plan, a plan to make me see what an idiot I've been to...to... Listen, ahh, are you in your office?"

Three minutes later she stepped into my office, looking flushed. She closed the door. "Bob and I had a tremendous fight last night. When you asked me to go out with you, I realized what a farce it was that I couldn't just say yes, in front of him. Like he owns me, or something. So I told him I want to see other guys. He started in about the divorce thing again, and I told him to forget it, that it wouldn't work, that I didn't want the responsibility. He accused me of conspiring with you to set this whole thing up. I thought you had planned it that way."

"I'm not that smart."

She paused, confused. "Then, you really just wanted to go out with me?"

I didn't have to answer. I was back on that dry savannah, having slain the alpha male. I pulled her to me roughly and kissed her. She resisted a little at first, then I felt her melt. After the second kiss we gathered up our things and drove to my apartment.

We stood in the kitchenette, sipping the rest of the Chardonnay from the bottle, kissing tentatively, unable to look too long in each other's eyes. I put *The Gypsy Kings* on the CD, but it was too raucous, and I turned it low. She kicked off her loafers, stood in front of the bay window looking out over Noe Valley, undid her skirt and slipped it off, then her blouse. I came up behind her and put my arms around her waist, kissed her neck, smelled her damp skin. She didn't move. My body began to hurt everywhere. "It's not right, is it?" I said. She didn't answer. "You love him, don't you?" She lowered her head. "It's okay," I said, "whatever's right will happen." She undid her bra, slipped it off, turned around, and embraced me, mechanically. The pain soared.

In bed we were serious, thoughtful, even respectful, the way we'd always been at the office, until pleasure began to take hold, and we laughed, but then the quiet came down around each one of us, separately. "I really wanted to know," she said, and I began to cry, hiding my face.

I wanted to hear her voice say the words. I wanted to open myself to her, to pour out all the horror of the past months, tell her the whole story about the *domhain comharthai* and the flashbacks, but I kept quiet. Stroking her back and bottom as she lay on her stomach, I did tell her I had come to the end of an era in my life, that the vision I had been working on for several years had dissolved, leaving only an urgent need, a command, to change. She wanted to know why, but I suspected that the answer wouldn't really be of much use to her, even if she understood it, which I doubted as well.

"I'll tell you something about myself that I'm not especially proud of, something that I know has always added difficulty to my life, but something I can't change about myself," I said. "What's always mattered most to me is not people, or places or anything I can look at and say, This is mine. There are people I love here, I love this town, I feel lucky to live here and have this job. But these things have never defined me. What defines me is something abstract. Some people might call it a vision, or a set of ideas or principles, but that's not really it either. It's a sense of harmony, a fit between what I believe… No. Wait. 'Believe' isn't the right word, it's too intellectual. A fit between what I *intuit,* what *makes sense to me,* and the way I live. I don't pretend to know more than other people, or to be better than them. I only have this…this extreme sensitivity, like a musician's ear, to what does, or doesn't harmonize with who I am. Does that make any sense at all?"

"And now you feel the way you're living doesn't make any sense? How long have you known this?"

"It's crept up on me in the last few months, since I came back from Ireland. I know what caused it, but I can't explain it to you right now."

"So the Morse Brulay I just slept with is not the person I've known all along? Actually, I sensed that, starting yesterday. Does it have anything to do with me?"

"You've played a part in it, but it would've happened anyway, if I didn't know you."

"Why can't you tell me?"

I thought for a moment. "It's too much to expect someone, a normal person, to understand. It has to do with shamanic experiences. I've studied shamanism for many years now. I've worked with shamans, I've learned their methods. Shamanic thinking isn't something you can explain to people, even superbly intelligent people like you, it's deeply different. Even my understanding is very rudimentary."

"I've read *The Teachings of Don Juan*," she said. "Is that what you're talking about?"

"Do you feel you understood it?"

"Not really. Did you?"

"I understand that Castañeda made most of that up, but the real thing is no easier to understand, believe me."

"I heard your Spring Lecture. You're quite good at explaining things."

I shook my head. "I'm not ready to risk telling anybody. Maybe some day."

"I feel left out now."

"I've let you farther in than anybody already. No one else knows I'm leaving."

"That's cause you haven't seen anybody but me since you decided, isn't it?"

"That's true, but that's not why." We were quiet then, so as not to awake the sleeping dragon of the question, How far did this go? What was the shape of it? I wanted her to be mine so desperately, but the thought of saying it panicked me. I sensed that that she wanted to be friends, and the thought made me ill. I forced myself to relax a little. When you don't know what to do, don't do anything. We got up and dressed, she kissed and embraced me the way a sister would, and she left.

When I got to my office the message light on my phone was blinking. It was time for us to talk about what had happened, and what had not happened. I pushed the voice mail button. The message was from someone else. I erased it without listening, then dialed Celine. "Can you meet me somewhere tonight?"

There was a pause. "Can we wait a while? I need time to think."

"Celine, this is very heavy for me. I can't stand here and hold it. Anyway, I have to make decisions."

"Talk to me then."

"I…I'll stay here if…if you want me to. Otherwise—" I was cursing myself as the words and the tears came out.

"You know I can't ask that." We were silent for a while, then she said, "Morse, I'm so grateful, so deeply grateful that you think you love me. But I think if it wasn't me it'd be someone, or something, else. Think about what you told me in bed. You've lost your footing, your connection to everything, you're drifting, you're reaching for something, anything, an anchor. Oh, God, I wish I'd known, before I made it worse for you."

"Don't start blaming yourself."

"I admire you so much. I'll always remember this day. You may not believe it right now, but you gave me something really beautiful, okay?"

"Yeah. Okay. Listen, I'll call you before I leave."

"Okay. Everything will turn out, I know it will."

"Bye."

"Bye."

I sat there and shook, my brain an anthill of unconnected oddities. I got up and rushed out of the building, across the campus, through the town, until I found myself on a cliff among twisted cypress trees, looking out over a restless sea, a lone gull hovering on the wind just below me. As I scanned the horizon my mind began to clear. Was Celine right, was my need for her simply the need to value something, anything, to fill the hole that the flashbacks had torn in my ethos? I thought of Nietzsche, "Esteeming itself is of all esteemed things the most estimable treasure." Was this the lesson that the *fomors* meant to beat into me, that the scruples of the mortal world are nothing but opiates? Indeed the *fomor* Dryr had railed against heroes and saints. Well, for now they seemed to have made their point. A beautiful woman gives herself to a starving man, so that she can find out whether she really loves another. I looked down at the eternal, unchanging sea, which said, "Come on, join the legion of idiots who've thrown themselves here for nothing, for want of a word or a name to scratch on a wall."

Thank you *fomors,* thank you sea, thank you Celine. Where to begin, then? I had savings and didn't have to work for months, or even years if I stayed on the cheap. I had skills—teaching, writing, speaking. I could find work almost anywhere, but what I craved was simplicity, a place where life was elemental, where people were born, ate, slept, fought, danced, copulated, and died, without calling it something else. A place, in other words, where few people read or write or use cars or TVs or telephones or banks. Nepal? Ladakh? Too cold. Indonesia? The Philippines? I don't speak those languages, but I can get by in Spanish. South America, then. The Peruvian Amazon. I had studied the intricate shamanic lore of the Yanomami, the Jivaro, the Bororo, the Sharanahua, and I understood it, admired it.

The Amazon it was, then.

Chapter Eight

Amazonia

It was early on a June morning, the dry season. We beached the canoe on a stretch of sand where the waters of the Marañón River had receded near the Kurudahé village of Tukos. The motor now silent, we could hear the chorus of chirps, whistles, squawks, hoots, and chirrs from the great green labyrinth in front of us, punctuated now and then by the deep thunderous roar of a red howler monkey. With a languid energy unaffected by the biting flies, my Kurudahé guide, Masanch, helped our guests unload their bundles, then shepherded them into a safe place in the shade, warning them against the thorns on a palmito. A boy-sized athlete in his middle age, Masanch was always aware of the great gap between his own powers of perception (and action) and those of his white clients in the jungle. At first I had found this annoying, an implication that I was fragile or inept; but by now I understood his personality. Masanch was the jungle version of a detail person, someone who enjoyed a job he could take seriously and perform methodically and well. We watched him now as he turned the largest canoe upside down and beat on it with a small flat rock for about a minute. It made an excellent log-drum, a sound that could be heard for miles in the jungle. It was best not to arrive silently in this part of the Amazon.

Our guests were a middle-aged couple from Madrid and their daughter-in-law. All of them field biologists, they were strong and competent, and at once set about putting up the canvas lean-tos and mosquito nets while Masanch brought dry firewood from one of the canoes and started a fire. The sun was scorching now, but clouds were blowing in from the Andes and it would very soon be pouring as it can pour only here in this endless deep sea of vegetation.

We cooked and ate a couple of fish that Masanch had speared from the canoe, then filled our pots with the coals, and set them inside the mosquito nets to relieve the cold as the rain drummed on the tarps over us. It softened into a dreary mist after about two hours, and soon after that Tirineh and Ukupi appeared. These two Kurudahé men I knew well were carrying blowguns and bows and a loosely woven basket with a couple of small monkeys and a macaw for their families' dinner. They looked like brothers, both short, with wiry frames and bland, handsome faces. Along with the usual feather and bone ornaments in their nasal and lower lip piercings, they both wore slightly ragged shorts and T-shirts. Their lack of face paint meant that they put no special importance on our meeting.

"I'm happy to see you, *ihaichne,"* I said as we embraced, using the Kurudahé term for cousins. Masanch translated our Spanish as we spoke. "These are my *ihaichne* from far away," I went on, "Don Paolo and Doña Francesca, and this is their daughter Lilia."

"We haven't seen you since the beginning of the rainy season," said Tirineh. "Did you go to Iquitos?"

"I went there," although the truth was, I had gone all the way to Lima. I doubted that they had ever taken the 300-kilometer canoe trip to Iquitos or would know where Lima was.

"What did you bring?" Ukupi asked, getting right down to business.

"Medicine, shotgun shells, batteries." These were things I knew the traders who bought their hides would not bring, preferring to trade in rum and clothing. I hoped the one boom box here still worked, as I also had four CDs recorded in Iquitos by singers of this region.

"Tobacco?" asked Ukupi.

"*Ihaichne,* the tobacco of Tukos is the best there is."

"You say you have none? You're lying, *Ihaichne Ekeja,*" said Ukupi. "You only share your tobacco with your foreign cousins, never with us."

As Masanch translated, I turned to Don Paolo and explained, "Calling someone a liar in Kurudahé is not an insult. It's one of the things they accept about people they like." Nodding, Don Paolo fished in his bundle and brought out a pack of Spanish cigarettes, which Ukupi opened slowly and ceremoniously, and offered around before lighting one for himself with a brand from the coals.

"We will stay here hands and feet," I told them, meaning more than ten days. "My dear *ihaichne* here come from a land far beyond Iquitos. In the place where they live are no pacas or jaguars, no anacondas or tree frogs or howler monkeys. They will not hunt these things, nor anything that lives here. They only want to learn from them. You see? They brought their food in boxes."

The men laughed. "But they're women! Do they drink *natem?"*

I turned to the biologists. "Women cannot see the spirits of the animals, so they think it's funny that you want to learn about them. *Natem* is their word for the hallucinogen you know as ayahuasca, the medicine that allows the men to see the spirits, and to understand their songs." Turning to Ukupi and Tirineh I said, "They have a way to speak with the spirits without *natem.*"

"Teach us this way, then."

"If you began to learn now, you would not finish before your son was grown. My dear *ihaichne* from far away must go back to their family in a few days."

"Why does it take so long to learn it? Surely our *natem* is much better than their medicine." They turned to go.

"Come back tomorrow with your brothers," I called. Then to the biologists, "They'll bring meat and steamed manioc, and expect to share our food. Don't worry, monkey makes a nice change from crackers and tuna fish. They'll help us carry our things to the village."

Our beach was bathed with a strange orange light as the sun dipped below the clouds, hovering over the darkening green sea of treetops. The mosquitoes began to appear and we retreated to our net structure to plan the excursions of the next few days.

"I'm beginning to see why you have quite a reputation as a guide," Doña Francesca said. "How long have you been doing this?"

"About three years."

"Is that all? What did you do before?"

"I taught psychology at an American university. That lifestyle came to seem somehow fake to me, all the egotism and posturing. I wanted to get away from so-called civilization."

"I thought maybe some great tragedy."

I shook my head.

"What was it the Indians called you? Elijah?"

"Oh. Ekeja. It means a white beetle grub. A reference to my skin color, and a joke about my eating habits."

"You know these people very well, then."

"It would be impossible to bring clients to this stretch of the jungle without the friendship of a local community. This enormous valley, the basin of the Marañón, is the ancient property of many peoples, and all of them dislike strangers. Our agency specializes in expeditions that are long, remote, and difficult."

"Of course. Your agency, Tropic Field Science, is elite. That's why we chose you. But what makes you so good at it?"

"That's hard to explain. The short answer is, I admire them. They're my kind of people. Human beings can pretty much tell when they're liked and when they're not. Also, my clients and the local people have a lot in common. You respect the forest, you study it, learn from it. And you accept hardship."

Every morning we rose before daylight, in order to reach the deep jungle as the sun came up. The biologists were astonished by Masanch's knowledge of the area. As we pushed through the undergrowth or waded across the palm swamps, he would suddenly stop and raise his hand to his ear, a signal for quiet. We would strain our ears and eyes fruitlessly as we crept after him until, without fail, he would point to something through the dense foliage—a tapir, a sloth, a peccary, a capybara. I was also aware that he knew the songs and could call the spirits of many animals, but he never did this openly.

After eight days the biologists' notebooks and sample jars were filling up; but their keenest wish remained unfulfilled. They wanted to find a particular rare species of fruit bat, reported only in the Marañón River basin, a very large bat that locates its food by smell, then crashes into the foliage at alarming speed to seize it. The biologists wanted DNA samples, to discover whether it was actually related to the flying foxes of Melanesia. It was certain that the Kurudahé knew of it, they described its habits and called it *kinita*. However, the bat was so rare that no one in the village had seen, much less spoken to, its spirit, which explained why we could not find it. Evidently the *natem* of the foreigners was not up to the task, it would be necessary or them to drink the local variety—or rather, for Don Paolo and me to do so, as it is not women's business.

It was decided. On the tenth night, we would go to Tukos village, where the shaman Mitiswangi had cut and boiled the bark of the *natem* vine, and was ready to lead us with his singing into the trance, in search of the spirit of *kinita*.

I myself had drunk *natem* several times, so that morning in the shade of our lean-to I instructed Don Paolo in the basics.

"Drink the whole bowlful straight off. It's extremely bitter, and you have to drink a good deal of it to get the effect. At first the sensation will be chaotic, dancing lights and colors and jumbled sounds. You'll soon be overcome with nausea. Don't resist vomiting, it's part of the process. Then, you'll begin to see and feel snakelike forms, coiling and writhing inside you. This can be quite frightening, but if you listen carefully to Mitiswangi's songs, you'll be calmed. This might be all that happens your first time, but still, it's important that you do this—it shows respect for their magic and their beliefs. Anyway, if you're very lucky, luckier than I've ever been, you'll start to see small humanlike figures dressed in bright costumes. These are the spirits of nature, the *aroe*. You can converse with them. It doesn't matter what language you use, as their understanding is universal. Ask them about *kinita*, where you can find him. It may be that you will have a dream later on, with the answer to your question."

"Do you believe these things?"

I thought for a moment. "There are so many things in this world that you and I don't understand, so much that we have never allowed ourselves to experience. I can tell you this: The Kurudahé understand some things, some very profound and powerful truths, that we Westerners lost and forgot when we turned to monotheism, and then to science."

"What kinds of things?"

"Time, for example. The *aroe* spirits live in a world free of time, in a dimension where past and future coexist. Your ancestors and mine used to know these same spirits by other names, but we've forgotten. It's not simply an illusion. I've studied the world of these spirits for many years—here and in New Guinea, among the Druids of Ireland, among the Native American people of my country. The spirits are the same, and they've shown me glimpses of their world."

At dusk we made our way to the village. A ring of some twelve men sat on logs around a fire, some of them smoking cigars of the native tobacco. Next to the fire sat Mitiswangi, smoking tobacco, singing the sweet, melodic *natem* chant, and pouring out drafts into the men's gourds, which they promptly drank. Don Paolo and I followed suit, and I was quickly lost in the trance. I had by this time overcome the fear of the snake-forms, which now seemed to enter me playfully, their iridescent coils inviting me to a pleasant place where the men around me, and in fact the whole jungle and its countless inhabitants, were brothers. In my trance I heard Don Paolo groaning from time to time, and saw Tirineh and Ukupi stroke his head with tobacco leaves, to ease his suffering. I was keenly aware of Mitiswangi's singing, to which my visions seemed to dance; and at times I had flashes of "normal" consciousness, in which I compared this to other shamanic journeys, and even to science fiction films I had seen. Curiously, I remained aware of where I was, who else was there, what I was doing, and how much time had passed.

After some hours, we all went down to the Marañón to bathe in the cool water and listen as the exotic whispers inside us and those out in the tree canopy gradually separated themselves and became distinct, as if the *aroe* were saying goodnight and dancing back to their haunts. It occurred to me that the Druidic *fomors* were certainly among them, and the thought made me strangely happy. It was as if the gentle presence of the *aroe* (who, to be sure, could delude and afflict as well as heal and guide) were guaranteeing me safe passage among all spirits everywhere. Come to think of it, I hadn't had one of my flashbacks in many months.

The next morning we sat resting in the deep shade where the stream passes behind the communal hut, drinking coffee, listening to the water and the distant, steady thud of women pounding manioc in their mortars. Don Paolo laughed and said that he had seen more biology in one night—and closer at hand—than in his entire career. "I don't know what I learned," he said, "other than the narrowness of my life and my science. I'm beginning to understand your fascination with these people. This Mitiswangi, if he were to take his show on the road, the so-called civilized world might find him irresistible. And then there's Masanch. What accounts for his impressive confidence, his deep calm in all situations? I almost wonder if he really does have some magic formula that makes him invincible, that guarantees him a kind of success at everything."

"Maybe it's just because he sticks to what he knows," Francesca said, looking at me.

Chapter Nine

The Bow

I thought for a moment. "I'll tell you a story about Masanch and Mitiswangi that might shed a small ray of light on their knowledge system—maybe on all knowledge systems, for that matter. One day a couple of years ago, before I knew him well, Masanch and I were leading a pair of bird biologists from Maryland around the clay licks up here. Masanch would disappear into the forest for hours at a time, and come back with a branch or two of hardwood, which he would heat over the fire for a bit, examine carefully, and discard. I figured he was planning to make a bow or some such implement, but he didn't explain it to me, and I didn't ask. Eventually he kept two of these, and carried them with him. We got back to Tukos a couple of days before a *natem* gathering, and at the gathering I noticed that he had brought the two branches with him, along with a bundle of river stones, bird and animal bones, herbs, and arrow points. In the forest a little ways off from the clearing where the men were gathered, he let me watch while he carefully built a complex altar of these things, and laid the branches on it before he drank the *natem,* squatting in front of it and singing the trance song.

"I took *natem* also, so I didn't notice what he did after that, but the next day I saw that he had only one branch, and that he had begun to shape it into a traditional Kurudahé bow. He took his project with him on our forays to the clay licks, and over the next couple of weeks he would sit working on it while the bird men set up their tripods and clicked away. When he finally put the string on it, I commented that it was a beautiful piece of work, and he handed it to me. It looked exactly like an ordinary bow, except that the wood was a pale gold, in contrast to the usual darker color. When I hefted it, I felt that it was a bit lighter and pulled a bit easier than the usual ones, too. To my surprise I could pull it without trembling, or anyway not much. For a second I thought he might have meant it for me, but he took it back, and I didn't see it for several months.

"I had forgotten all about the bow, until one day I was with a hunting party of Kurudahé that included Masanch, Mitiswangi, Tirineh, and Ukupi, and two other men. We had to cross a small, swift stream without a boat, and the men tied their blowguns, arrows, darts, and game in bundles to carry on their heads, slinging their bows around their shoulders. Mitiswangi alone had not shot anything, so his bundle was the smallest and lightest, but I saw that Masanch stayed close to him. I guessed because he was older and smaller than the others. We had to move slowly and backtrack a few times, groping for footing. All at once, in the middle of the stream, Mitiswangi began shouting and thrashing the water with his arms, and I thought he had lost his footing; but I saw that he still had his gear bundle on his head, and we continued to the opposite bank. There was great commotion when we reached dry ground, and I learned that Mitiswangi had lost his bow—apparently the string had broken, and the current quickly carried it away. The men tried to console him, as he was beside himself, and continued to wail and curse into the night after we had returned to the village. A Kurudahé's bow is almost part of his body, certainly part of his personality.

"The next day we went out again, and this time, I noticed that Mitiswangi was carrying a yellow bow, which I recognized as the one Masanch had made with such care. The old shaman had good luck that day, bagging a small peccary, and it didn't take me long to put the pieces together. Mitiswangi had not been successful hunting lately, probably because his old bow was too much for his aging arm. I don't have to tell you, it is typical of Masanch that he noticed this and took an action that would solve the problem without humiliating his friend."

"Masanch must have cut the string on Mitiswangi's old bow," Paolo mused. "But what does this tell us, except what a fine person our guide is?"

"Mitiswangi is an adept shaman," I said. "He is intimate with the *aroe*, he knows the songs of the game. Such a man should be a great hunter, right?"

"Of course."

"Knowledge alone is not enough. It supplements skill, technology, and character."

"I get skill and technology," Francesca said. "Are you talking about Masanch's character, too?"

"No. Mitiswangi's. He certainly saw through the bow story as easily as I did, and he had to accept it graciously."

Paolo shook his head gravely. "That must have been tremendously hard for him."

Francesca frowned. "What amazes me is that Masanch *knew* Mitiswangi would accept it, or he would not have taken that risk."

"I suppose this is the sort of thing people in small societies know about each other," Paolo said, fixing me with a knowing smile.

Chapter Ten

Principles

Two days later Tirineh, Ukupi, a few other Kurudahé men helped us carry our gear to the canoes, we said good-bye and slipped with the swift current of the Marañón back toward Iquitos. We never did get a glimpse of the bat, *kinita*. Maybe its *aroe* had taken a look at us that night and decided against a rendezvous. Coming back to the city, I always had mixed emotions. It was great to take a shower, to sleep in a bed, to read a newspaper. But Iquitos' wild stew of accents, music, and costumes, like the honking, swerving traffic in the narrow streets, soon began to chafe my nerves. On my way to the office of Tropic Field Science, I gave a few coins to an elderly blind man in a coat and tie playing *jotas* rather badly on a guitar. A few steps later I sidestepped an adolescent whore in jaguar tights and was almost flattened by a dowager driving an ancient Rolls. Near my office I declined a set of pink grass place mats waved at me by a Yanomami family wearing bone labrets and face paint. Our tiny office was housed in the Hotel Pescadero, and as I walked through the lobby I cast an envious eye on the young clerk, slumped asleep with a copy of *Futbol Mundo* in his lap.

Being the owner of the "elite" Amazon tours agency allowed my boss, Jaime, to indulge in certain eccentricities. Although many agencies keep parrots or monkeys in their offices as symbols of their exotic profession, Jaime's symbol was an anaconda big enough to swallow at least an adult goat. Usually draped over his desk and person, Ruby, as he called her, was thoroughly tame, and she did serve a purpose. People waiting in the office would often fixate on her for up to an hour, hoping to see her move. She had a disconcerting habit of sleeping with her head in Jaime's pants pocket, which, if you had any imagination, created a rather fantastic illusion. Today, Jaime's excitement stood in stark contrast to Ruby's profound relaxation. He looked me up and down as if he had never seen me before. "Do you know who Señor Richard Parkbourne is?"

"The name sounds vaguely familiar. A personage, I assume?"

"President of the WDF."

"The World Development Fund? Do we owe them money?"

"Don't be funny, we're not the Ministry of Finance. Señor Parkbourne himself phoned me from their headquarters in New York. Yes. I spoke with him. He wants you to take him into the Amazon." Jaime's face shone like a new coin.

"Why doesn't he ask the Minister of Finance?"

"This is serious, Morse. He has heard about your reputation as a guide, and he insists no one else will do. There are two others with him. We can't take them in our canoes of course, we'll have to charter..."

"Wait a minute. We specialize in scientific tours. What does Richard Proctor plan to do in the jungle?"

"Parkbourne. He's known as a man of great ideas." Jaime shoved a copy of *El Economista* at me. "He has a plan to save the rain forest with a tremendous tourism project."

I looked at the newspaper, then at Jaime. "Since when were you a fan of the WDF? You know the sorts of projects they support."

"Yes, yes, the dams, the nuclear power. In the papers, the environmentalists are always cursing them. But Parkbourne recognizes what they say. He's gone green. He wants to help Peru develop our economy in an eco-friendly way."

"Jaime, look at their record. Their policy couldn't be more clear, it's to push the exploitation of resources for profit. Sure, their projects now have green trimmings. Be careful not to pollute the area with mine tailings—but by all means dig that mine. When you build that dam and flood the river valley, make sure the farmers don't go up in the hills and cut down the forest—but by all means build that dam. Put the oil pipeline on stilts so the caribou can cross under it—but by all means pump that oil. Do they monitor the effects of their projects once they're built? Do they make sure the local communities, the ones who've cared for the land for centuries, share in the benefits? I'm sorry, but I won't have anything to do with the WDF. I won't work with Parkbourne."

Jaime jumped to his feet, causing Ruby to rearrange her coils. "You what? Do you know what you're saying? Any agency in Iquitos—any agency in the world, would *kill* to get the WDF, let alone Señor Richard Parkbourne himself! You can't just say you won't do it!"

"Jaime, remember our agreement when you hired me? We both said we would try this out, to see whether it worked for both of us. Well, it seems to have worked, up to now. I like you. I can do a good job because I find nothing offensive about my work or my clients. I find the WDF highly offensive, which means I couldn't do a good job for them, and as I refuse to do a lousy job, I refuse to work for them at all. And you'd better take Ruby off your keyboard before she creates her own Facebook page." Unnoticed, Ruby was now slithering across Jaime's computer, causing it to make frantic beeping sounds.

Ignoring her, Jaime leaned across his desk and narrowed his eyes. "Have you considered the possibility that you would be in a unique position to influence Señor Parkbourne's plans?"

"I don't want to influence his plans."

"Hah! You are afraid of him!"

The phone rang and Jaime's attention was absorbed by the call, and by trying to retrieve a sheaf of papers lying under Ruby's main coil. I began to feel a familiar nausea and dizziness, and then:

My squire Gottlieb at my side, my sheriff and his two secretaries close behind, I follow the palace guardsmen through the arch of the castle gate and up the marble steps to the meeting chamber. It isn't much of a castle—three levels of yellow granite with a little tracery around the doors. The prince is very proud of the garden, full of the new thing, what's it called? Tulips? Well, the tulips seem to be his only friends; even his wife's family has refused him a share of their vineyards along the Rhine. I'm here today because he knows he cannot fight the French without my company of men.

He is a large man, but soft. I feel embarrassed, to see him dressed in gold-embroidered silk and lace, the style our enemy has stamped all over Christendom. At least he isn't wearing a powdered wig, although he seems to allow this, too, among the chancellery staff around him.

"Captain von Nidda," he greets me, stressing my military title but mispronouncing my name. I kneel to kiss his hand, and he pulls me up, explaining, "All German-speakers are brothers in this terrible time."

Aha. He's going to ask me to join the Protestant Knights. "Do you include the Lutherans, Your Highness?"

"A sinner might still be saved if the Lord approves his works, von Nidda. Sir Severne may not be willing to embrace us in his heart, but he will welcome any German to his side."

I keep silent.

"Only if we join Severne can we save Grotzheim," the prince goes on. "He has a strong force."

I turn sick and cold at the thought, but not from fear. Behind their public air of piety, the Evangelicals hide an overweening pride. With their wild tracts against our priests, they struggle to seduce our neighbors and our children away from the true Church. Sneeringly they talk of the wealth and power of Rome as if it were a symbol of corruption, rather than proof of the Lord's favor. They prattle constantly of brotherhood but lock themselves indoors rather than enjoy the beauty and tradition of our festivals.

I kneel and cross myself. Closing my eyes I wait for a word, a sign, but hear only the coughing and foot shuffling of those around us. I look up at the prince's round, serious face. "The valiant men of Grotzheim will stand with you and the princes of the One True Church, Your Highness. I cannot ask them to jeopardize their souls."

"The French are burning the fields and towns of all German faiths on their way down the Rhine. If we do not join Severne, and, yes, the other Protestant knights, everyone here will suffer worse than what our grandfathers bore in Alsace, believe me."

"Then we will die with honor, Sire."

The flashback faded and I stood again in Jaime's office. The scene around me now seemed like a painting by Dalí, or a story by Kafka, far less real than the one I had just visited. Jaime stood with his cell phone in one hand while wrestling the boa with the other. He seemed to be discussing food preferences with a client. Meanwhile his employee—me—had refused on principle to follow his orders. On principle, on belief. I had failed, after all, to learn the lesson that had brought me here, the lesson of the *fomors,* that belief itself, the habit of believing, divorced from the raw pursuit of existence, is nothing but corrosive illusion. I waited until Jaime hung up the phone, then I said, "You're right, *Mi Jefe.* I'm not afraid of Parkbourne. When does he want to start?"

Chapter Eleven

Salvation

The rivers of the Amazon are the least predictable of living things. Weekly they shift their courses, cutting away a bank here, raising a sandbar there, changing a calm deep into a boiling rapid or swirling eddy. Their levels rise and fall by several feet in the course of a day; their colors change, their currents quicken and slack, and during the frequent violent rains, it's impossible to read their depth or current, or to see at any distance the masses of vegetation and huge tree trunks that hurry along their courses, get stuck on their shoals, sink, and re-emerge. I was glad to have Masanch steering our little launch up the Marañón from Iquitos. Intent but relaxed at the outboard's tiller, he read the current and picked his route from moment to moment the way a pro running back might pick his way through a dangerous defense.

Oblivious to the drama, Richard Parkbourne sat in the bow with his iPod in his ears and his delicate hands conducting a ghost orchestra. Mahler was his favorite, he said. At first I wondered whether he was even aware of the river and the jungle around him, but when we tied up the first evening I learned that he was indeed. There were five of us; the slender, elegant Parkbourne with his horn-rimmed glasses; Yukichi, his economist, short and stocky with his straight black hair pulled back in a pony tail, Lotte, his enthusiastic blonde biologist, thirtysomething and athletic; my guide Masanch; and myself. The tin-roofed trading shack where we stopped leaned on its stilts as if trying to wade into the river, away from the crowding green forest. The heat was impressive and the mosquitoes thick around its rotting dock, yet Parkbourne looked as comfortable as if we were sitting in the lobby of the Lima Hilton. "That last outpost we passed, that was Tishimpu, wasn't it?" he asked.

"That was Tishimpu, yes." Not many visitors would have known that.

"When rubber ruled the jungle and the tropics were ambition's dream," he went on, "it was a little boom town, I believe. The local people—the Aguaruna, isn't it?—still have the mixed blessing of missionary schools."

"You've done your homework."

"How do they regard the wide-eyed visitor from afar?"

"Tourists? These local communities have a long history of conflict with outsiders, even with other communities that share their culture. Spanish speakers are to be given wide berth."

"They gird their loins against the coming oil and timber hordes," he mused. "They could use some modern allies, could they not?"

"You have thoughts about that, I imagine."

"Coarse, clumsy thoughts, yes. Our ideas need polishing. Help us to become geographers, ethnographers, ecologists, Professor Brulay."

Professor Brulay. He was telling me that I had been researched as well. "In two weeks?" I snorted.

Parkbourne smiled. "We stand on the shoulders of midgets," he said. His damned self-confidence unnerved me. As president of a global bank, he had almost certainly dealt with *fomors.* He might know some of them personally. It even crossed my mind that he might *be* a *fomor,* but that seemed far-fetched and I shook it off.

We set up camp in a clearing near the trading post. Our rented boat had refrigeration, and we dined well on fresh fish and greens, sitting on hammocks under the group mosquito net while I briefed the group on the lands and cultures of the upper Marañón. Yukichi, whom I'd seen puffing on a bong before dinner, looked a bit spacey, his eyes red, his pupils dilated. He had the annoying habit of muttering to himself in Japanese while I spoke; but finally in the dim light I saw that he was recording into a tiny headset. Lotte rose from her hammock and sat down cross-legged with a laptop on her knees, now and then stopping her note taking to throw Parkbourne an admiring smile. She was one of those gracefully long-limbed northern women with the ivory skin that easily turns golden brown in the sun, the blue eyes, the thick straight honey blonde hair cut short and washed daily. Even spattered with mud and dark with sweat, the khaki jumpsuit she wore looked superb on her small-breasted, full-hipped body.

For his part Parkbourne, who alone seemed entirely comfortable and composed in the steamy heat, plied me with questions. How far up the Pastaza, the Marañón, the Santiago, can you take a motor launch? What Kurudahé food might North Americans like? What handicrafts could be produced from native materials? I could see the direction of his questioning, and I began to feel queasy about what I was doing. "Mister Parkbourne," I said at length, "the people of this forest are my colleagues in this small but sustainable enterprise—my friends, in fact. We respect each other. I bring them things that help them sustain their way of life—simple clothes, hand tools. Your questions point in a direction that's worse than completely foreign to them. The people are an intimate part of a fragile community of living things. To make these river lands inviting to foreigners, you'd have to completely destroy their way of life. You're an educated man. I'm sure you understand what I'm saying."

"Ah, yes, their way of life. The balance of the ecosystem. Half of what you say, and the feeling behind it, is glorious truth. In the hands of egomaniacs and fools, our technology is a threat more deadly than cancer to the body of nature. But we have learned that now, and we come in search of a cure."

"Yes," said Lotte, her pale eyes glistening in the lamplight. Her alto voice with its touch of accent rang with the tense energy of aroused idealism. "Thank God we have learned it. With all our might, we must use everything we know now to go back, undoing and undoing, until the wisdom of the Kurudahé becomes a part of our wisdom, too—"

"And ours becomes part of theirs," Parkbourne interrupted. "At one time your ancestors and mine, by wit and brawn, coaxed a hard living from a fragile forest too. Were they better off, then? Were they? Each new trembling step in the great dance of history, as soon at it's taken, creates a new future, an unimagined future. We can't go back, even if we want to, and we can't stand still." As he spoke the graceful motions of his long hands made oversized shadows from the lamplight flit around us.

"You speak of 'back' and 'forward,' as if history, as if time itself, was a…a garden path," I said. "I know I sound self-righteous, but this idea is one of the most destructive of all our modern conceits. Our own poor, unwashed ancestors knew better; they had a wisdom that protected them from the suicidal arrogance of so-called progress. You think yourselves open-minded for considering that these 'primitives,' our hosts here in the jungle, can actually teach us something, but the thought contains the proof of its own vanity. We assume we've progressed far beyond them, and now we coyly admit we might have been a little hasty in some small ways."

"Ecotourism is now a science, Professor. Have you studied it? Your fine arguments might be honed yet finer if you did. We seek to manage *all* the resources of the destination—social and cultural as well as biological and economic. We seek to sustain, or even improve, the health, the beauty, the integrity of the original." With a sweep of his arm he took in the entire Amazon basin. "We know that indigenous communities have specific ways of nurturing the forest and each other; we bring their leaders into the process. No one gains from our enterprise unless the local people gain equally."

"And how do you measure that gain?" I asked. "You can improve a people's health, train them for moneymaking work, expose them to exciting ideas; but how do you measure what they will lose—the ancient integrity of their folkways, the ennobling beauty of their spiritual love affair with the forest?"

Still smiling, he leaned forward. "Well asked, Professor. We must let these very questions guide our research."

"And must you keep your distance until you have the answers? At what point will you 'bring them into the process'? Before you make the decision to invade their lives at all? Or after the money has been allocated, the business partners chosen, the schedules written?"

Yukichi leaned forward and slowly pulled off his headset. "Excuse me, Professor Brulay, can I ask you little bit personal question? Why you took this job? I am sure you know position of WDF. I don't think you are so interested in money, so...?"

"It's a fair question," I said. "I knew your mission of course. I realize I'm as arrogant in my way as your backers are. I suppose I thought we might learn a little something from each other."

Yukichi nodded, thoughtful. "You teach humility to World Development Fund." He paused and leaned back. "I think you have good idea." In the semidark I couldn't read his face. For a second I wondered what he'd been smoking in his bong and made a mental note to ask him for a hit next time.

Lotte had been studying me and nodding. "I think maybe we can. Learn from each other, I mean," she said.

"Those words can be our lullaby for tonight," said Parkbourne. "At dawn we begin our perilous and worthy labor, the great assault on the false gods of modernity."

I lay in my hammock listening to the night sounds of the forest, the sweet cacophony of chirps, chirrs, whistles, rustlings of the great primeval metropolis, and thought about quitting, turning the boat around and speeding with the current back to Iquitos. But then what? I would have gained nothing, nothing but my "honor," that sequined g-string of my tribe. Parkbourne and his crew would be back in a day, back with someone more accommodating that Professor Morse Brulay. No, I would have to do my best, if not to "teach humility to World Development Fund," at least to draw out the hidden horrors of its plan.

Every few days we would rise before dawn and motor to a new place along the river, often beaching the boat to wait out a passing downpour, or seeking refuge in the deep shade when the midday sun hammered on the water. Then we would wait, often for half a day, while Masanch practiced his diplomacy with the local people. Occasionally we would have to move on, but in most places we would be accompanied into the forest by a few young men. Masanch was always alert, steering us through thorns, low branches, tangled vines, huge spiderwebs; stopping us to point out a spider monkey, a blue morpho butterfly, an armadillo den. Lotte wielded her video camera and her sample bags, Yukichi his voice recorder and his GPS, and Parkbourne stayed close to me, mentally recording, so it seemed, my every word.

"A tiny island in a mighty sea," he said as we left a village of the Kandoshi people, accompanied by three hunters and two dogs. "A society of intimates. A round of work that seldom varies as much as the song of a cricket. Why don't they go mad?"

"The question of an urbane man," I said. "They don't get bored because life on this 'island' is as varied and as challenging for them as your life among the world's capitals is for you. Your reference to crickets is apt. Hear that chirping sound? They know what insect makes that chirp, what its habits are, where it nests, what species pursue it, what foods and medicines can be had from it, and how to imitate its call. Their lives are mingled with its life—the many times they used it to attract game, the stories their fathers told them about its origins, the songs their women sing about it, the time it multiplied and became a plague. They know which forest spirits are its allies, what spells will protect their manioc crops against it. Perhaps its ghostly avatar, seen in drug dreams, has told them priceless secrets about the spirit world. This is true of every sound they hear, and they hear many more than you or I, believe me." We walked for a while in silence. "There is no end of things that matter to their way of life in such a crowded place, and so, no end to learning."

"They might have great enthusiasm for teaching these things to us who know nothing of them, and for learning our knowledge as well."

"Their knowledge isn't a travelogue; it isn't a menu of TV nature shows, or the contents of a Boy Scout manual. It has evolved over millennia, an inseparable strand of a coherent way of life. They don't conceive of it independently of its uses, and why should they? To make it an intellectual exercise would diminish it tremendously, trivialize it."

"And yet, human beings are famously curious, and capable of learning anything, are they not, Professor?"

Our group had stopped. The dogs were pacing and sniffing around the base of a tall tree, and the hunters, looking up to its highest branches, were loading their blowguns with poison darts, softly singing the spirit song of their prey. Parkbourne and I saw nothing, but each hunter, holding his bamboo tube vertical, blew a dart, then waited, continuing to sing. Several seconds passed, then we heard a crash in the branches and the sizable body of a red howler monkey bounced into fern thicket twenty feet from us. The hunters stood still, and a few seconds later an even larger one landed next to the first. Without ceremony the men peeled strips from a nearby liana, tied each monkey's hands together, and used the loops thus formed as shoulder straps to carry the carcasses on their backs.

"You miss my point, Mister Parkbourne. Curious, yes. Capable, yes. That's just the problem. All human communities are attracted by novelty, indiscriminately. But introducing a new element, especially a powerful element like television, or motorbikes, into an ancient system is exactly like introducing a rapacious new species into an ecosystem. Catastrophic turmoil always follows. A kid with MTV loses interest in the wisdom of his parents. A kid with a motorbike or a cell phone is already beyond their influence."

"And yet the civilized world is even now aiming its high-tech blowguns at these forests. Which is better, the poison darts of uncontrolled contact, or a benign and carefully controlled development?"

"There's no such thing as controlled development. You yourself spoke of transformation. All missionaries see themselves as saviors, but thanks to them, the world's native cultures are becoming pathetic copies of ourselves, eager to sell their heritage for designer jeans and Coca-Cola. I'll tell you what's better: leaving them the hell alone."

Lotte and Yukichi had caught up with us and were listening. "Morse is right," Lotte said. "You have to introduce one small thing at a time, something that will harmonize with the way of life. Medicine, for example. They know how to cure with herbs, one simply gives them new herbs."

I shook my head. "Our medicine is already an integral part of an alien system. How can you justify giving them aspirin but not antibiotics? And if you give them antibiotics, you are giving them refrigeration, which takes a power source. Will you give them a power source but not light, not music, not power tools?" I stopped and faced them. "Don't you see? We *believe* in our way of life, just as they believe in theirs. But unlike them, we think the distinction between us is a *problem*, a *tragedy*. I tell you, it is not." As I turned and pushed through the wet greenery, following Masanch and the hunters along the faint trail, I heard Yukichi's rapid Japanese dictation and wondered what he was imagining I had said.

After eleven days we reached the Kurudahé. With his bottomless thirst for manioc beer and his ample supply of weed, Yukichi was a big hit with them. While drunk, he let Ukupi's wife cut his hair in the local inverted-bowl style, and when the men had painted his face he lacked only a nose ornament to pass as a pale-skinned member of the village. It was their custom to include strangers in the full moon hunting dance, and Yukichi did it so gracefully that it was lucky for everybody he couldn't interpret the women's love gestures. Meanwhile Lotte and the village children immediately fell for each other, and the little ones required her to come to the river with them every evening to play.

On the third afternoon Ukupi approached us as we returned from our jungle excursion and told us men that we were invited to drink *natem*. "Ah, yes, the hallucinogen ayahuasca. Botanically *banastereopsis,* isn't it?" said Parkbourne when Masanch had translated this. "Not for us, I'm afraid. Of course you've tried it, Professor?"

"Many times. I wouldn't refuse it if I were you; they'll remember that. Look, you've asked me where I get my insights into the indigenous view of life. Well, *natem* is the key, the defining experience. This is your chance to show that you're really serious about understanding them. Masanch will guide you, as will the shaman, Mitiswangi." We were all watching him closely, and at length he nodded. An axial moment, I thought.

"Yes, this Masanch," he smiled. "He has the instincts of a mother, doesn't he?"

"Or those of a shepherd," I said.

I took myself to a bamboo grove beyond the village garden plots and sat for more than an hour, going over in my mind every detail I could recall of the lore associated with the *natem* ritual, the songs, and the spirits. During the ritual, I would do my best to concentrate on Parkbourne, to see if I could influence his understanding in any way. I had no concrete idea how to do this, and to my own surprise I found myself praying—yes, literally reciting prayers—to the *fomors* for help.

After the sun went down we walked to the clearing away from the women and children where the men gather twice or three times a week for *natem.* Mitiswangi sat near the central fire smoking tobacco and chatting easily with the other men. At length he began to whistle a spirit song while blowing smoke into a great round gourd, and after several minutes he poured from it bowls of the red-orange brew, which he handed to about a dozen of us. Parkbourne held back at first, but Masanch squatted next to him and held out his bowl, nodding gently until he had downed the whole thing. Yukichi and I took two servings each, eliciting smiles and caresses from the other men. As the drug took effect, I did my best to concentrate my thoughts as I had planned, but although this aim would surface from time to time among my vivid visions, I soon became completely immersed in the uncontrolled dream journey.

It was unlike any other *natem* journey I had had. Only the most vivid moments have followed me back to waking consciousness, but this is the essence of what I saw and heard: Miniature human figures in brilliant costumes approached from the forest and stood motionless, gazing at me. I knew from the myths that these were the nature spirits, those ardently sought by the Kurudahé in their vision quests. They know the past and future, the causes of illness and crime, the seduction songs of animals, plants, fishes, and women. Now they receded into the jungle, and as I followed them in my dream we seemed to be climbing a steep path, higher and higher, passing the tops of the forest, passing waterfalls. At length we came to a cold, windy crag where we looked out to the west where the sun was setting over an enormous landscape. Below us I saw what I later could only describe as history, spread out on it. I thought I saw among the thousand scenes below me the hut of the Conklin and the *sidh* of Cuimhne and the tribal village where I had studied in New Guinea. The towns and beaches of my youth were there, and many other things from my past, both trivial and moving.

The lilting spirit song of Mitiswangi seemed to pull my vision into the scene, like a telescope. I was sure I recognized the palace of the prince of Baden, and the Bay of Hoydis where my tribe fought the Thergoes. I looked for the iron-age village where I blew my conch shell and shamed Engren; and the dry savannah where I killed the alpha male. They must have been there, but in the vast sea of time I couldn't find them, and the spirits were moving on. The path wound around to the other side of the crag, facing east, and below us spread a different teeming beehive of scenes that made no sense to me at all, but filled me with a sense of dread so horrible that I began to scream. At once black clouds rolled over us, and I saw nothing but felt myself drenched with rain. At length I realized that Mitiswangi and others were pouring something over me, singing, and rubbing me with herbs.

My awareness gradually returned to the clearing in the jungle. Mitiswangi sat in the center, swaying and singing tirelessly, while hoots and yelps occasionally arose from the circle of older men, including Masanch, sitting around him near the fire. One of the youths was in a whirling sort of dance, shaking his head and weeping; another was vomiting violently while two friends held him and stroked his head and back. Yukichi sat cross-legged in the middle of the circle, his head thrown back, his eyes closed. His round face, still painted with blue-black Kurudahé designs, registered awe, terror, disgust, and mirth by turns, accompanied by groans, gasps, giggles. I looked around for Parkbourne and finally found him, pale and wild-eyed, hanging onto Masanch's hand as if it were the tiller of a storm-tossed ship. When I approached him, Masanch shook his head and motioned me away. I sat near the fire and shivered with emotion until exhaustion overcame all of us, and one by one we drifted off to our quarters, or simply lay down and slept on the ground. Dawn was breaking in the treetops when Masanch and I half-carried Yukichi and Parkbourne back to their hammocks.

The sun was already high in the trees when I woke and instantly remembered my *natem* journey. At first it was a stew of images and feelings, but in the light of day and sobriety they began to settle into a realization. Why hadn't I seen this from the beginning? The powers of these forest spirits and those of the *fomors* are identical. Perhaps their very identities are the same. Kurudahé knowledge had led me by a sinuous path to the very center of the actual *domhain comharthai.*

But why? As I walked to the river to bathe, my mind circled around and around the question. Why? Had the spirits been eavesdropping on my conversations with Parkbourne? It seemed egomaniacal to think so, but wait! I stopped in my tracks. The knowledge of the Druids was almost gone, destroyed by the same bulldozing modernity that Parkbourne and his like were carrying like a deadly virus to the last vital centers of this knowledge. I had seen two ends of the spectrum. I had actually doubled back along the track of history. Could this have happened by chance? Absolutely not. The true purpose of my nightmare flashbacks was suddenly clear. The *fomors'* tricks had torn me loose from my habitual world and driven me here to the Kurudahé. My "error" at the *sidh* of Cuimhne had been part of the plan—the use of modern technology to break an ancient law.

On my way back from the river the clouds rolled up, I felt the first drops of a new downpour and ran back to our quarters, where I found Parkbourne and Yukichi staring silently out at the curtain of rivulets from the thatched roof. "Are you okay?" I asked.

"Yes, yes," Parkbourne said absently. "Sorry we haven't—"

"No, no," I said. It was clear that he was still deeply affected by the fearful labors of last night. "Rest. It's been a strenuous trip." I turned to Yukichi. Our eyes met and held. He smiled—a smile I'll never forget, a smile of recognition, one that sent a shiver through my body. Whatever *he* had seen on his *natem* journey had clearly worked some sort of transformation. His smile said he would tell me when the time was right. I went to search for the rest of our party, and I found them in the communal hut, Masanch translating while Lotte questioned the women and tried to enter their answers on her laptop. A dozen children skittered around her, scuffling for a seat on her knee, playing with her hair, squealing as they touched her keyboard and were gently pushed away.

As I entered she sighed and closed the laptop. "The children want me to take them to the river when the rain lets up," she said. "In Amsterdam nannies make twenty euros an hour for one child."

The night cleared and we walked together in moonlight magnified by its reflection on the gigantic whispering leaves of balsa trees. At the smaller children's urging Lotte stripped naked and slipped into the water, a laughing black silhouette against the silver current, and I had to close my eyes to keep my soul, reminded that some things are exactly what they seem, and glorious at that. At length I heard the tired voices coming up the bank, and we followed the small sure feet along the path toward the huts, slapping at the mosquitoes that were thick under the trees.

"What will become of these people?" she wondered.

"What do you wish for them?"

"A child's wish. Another million moonrises over the Marañón." We walked a few steps in silence. "That's what you wish, too, isn't it, Morse?—a child's wish?"

"A while back, Lotte, you spoke of the wisdom of the Kurudahé. This is it. For them, there's no need to wish. The future is here, all around us, the future and the past. We only need to learn how to see it, how to treat it. I care about the moon too, but what I care most about is this wisdom. To lose it would be like losing a whole magnificent species."

"But can *you* see this wisdom? Can you hold it in your mind's eye, the way I do the children and the moon?"

"Yes, I can see it."

"Please, tell me what it looks like."

I laughed, suddenly self-conscious. "Imagine you have a computer in your head. The computer is connected to a Web site where the entire past and future are stored, everything that has ever happened or ever will. There is an elaborate log-on procedure that takes years to learn, but if you learn it, you can access this site."

"Do you know the log-on?"

"I've seen samples of the site—"

"How? What did you see?"

"I'm sorry, I can't tell you any more about it. The whole business is very dangerous unless you have deep knowledge of the lore, as the Kurudahé shamans do, as true shamans everywhere do."

"And of course this is not taught—"

"At Oxford or MIT, because it would kick hell out of the myths of science, wouldn't it? Not to mention the Judeo-Christian thing."

"Your specialty is shamanism. I've read a couple of your papers. This is why you came here, isn't it?"

"Part of the reason."

"How can I believe you about this timelessness? You won't tell me what you know. You could be a madman."

"Believe whatever you like. You asked me what I wish for, remember?"

We walked in silence until we smelled the smoke and saw the fires of the huts, like lightning bugs among the towering shadows. She stopped and looked for a moment as if transfixed by the scene, then turned to me and said, "My God. The past, the future—" She shook her head violently, as if trying to clear it, and walked quickly toward the huts.

We were to leave the next morning, and the people of the village gathered at the big central house, where the women were roasting two peccaries and handing around gourds of freshly made manioc beer. The women and men were beautifully painted and wore bright feathers in their ears, their lips, their hair. Masanch and Yukichi were missing, and I knew something strange was going on. At length Masanch came and sat next to me, looking serious. "Don Yukichi will stay here," he said quietly, using the Spanish honorific.

"Stay here? You mean he's not coming with us in the morning?"

"Not coming," he smiled self-consciously. "I'm sorry. Don Yukichi gave me a very fine speech about it, but I did not understand him well. He said he would speak to you himself."

I turned to Parkbourne. "Did you know that Yukichi plans to stay here?"

"What? Stay here? This is beyond absurd!" He jumped to his feet. "Masanch, fetch Yukichi if you please."

Lotte covered her face with her hands and shook her head. "I had a feeling about this," she groaned.

At that moment Yukichi appeared and sat among our Kurudahé hosts on the other side of the fire. "Well?" said Parkbourne.

The fire crackled. Somewhere a dog barked. One of the small children ran to her mother, whimpering.

"My father was fourteenth abbot of Rokusonji Temple, in Gifu," he began. "I supposed to be number fifteen. You know, recite scriptures for ancestors, teach sayings of Buddha to temple kids. Ancient things, dead people, one small place. Pretending to read Sutras, really reading

Adam Smith, John Maynard Keynes. The world, the future. Beautiful! So excited! Kyoto University, MIT, then WDF. My mother crying, I guess. My father very quiet, peaceful, only asking if I found my way. Every time I said yes, yes, but I felt so ashamed; it was not true at all." He looked at me and smiled. "Anyway, last night I saw so many things, I don't know what. Saw mother and father, and his father, and his father, together a huge crowd of people, old people, smiling, saying, '*Okaerinasai, okaerinasai,* welcome back, welcome back.' My father asked, 'Did you find your way?' and I said, 'Maybe, maybe not!' and I felt happy, very huge happiness." Yukichi shook his head, laughing. "*Strange!* I don't understand! Anyway, I'm sorry, I make a lot of trouble for you, but have to stay here to find the reason." He held up his voice recorder. "I will translate everything up to now and send to you right away."

The women began handing around gourds of beer, the men talking, joking. Two little boys started wrestling for a seat on Lotte's lap. Parkbourne kept his usual calm. "Come with us, Yukichi," he said after a while. "We need your input. You can come back here whenever you like."

Yukichi shook his head. "Very sorry. Even I go with you, my mind, my spirit, stay here, not useful."

My three clients turned to look at me. "Yukichi," I said, "your father and mother, the souls of your people, they aren't dead, and they aren't in one small place; that was your mistake—a very modern mistake. They're alive and everywhere. They're the world and the future just as much as these children here. Your father always knew that, but he knew you had to discover it yourself. The *natem* is just a window where they can speak to you. You don't have to stay here, because now you know."

"Maybe come soon," Yukichi said. "Maybe not. Maybe go back Japan, don't know. Anyway, now have to stay, to study this."

I turned to Parkbourne and Lotte. "You know as well as I do what has happened to Yukichi. It's happened to you, maybe in smaller ways. You've realized how modernity fills us with a fear of the past, of the simple, the traditional. You've probably winced at the shallowness of planned obsolescence; the idea of endless progress has at times seemed ridiculous to you. You know there is another way of thinking, maybe more valuable. When you've touched the ancient, you've felt its power, known that part of what we've thrown away is the realization that all true knowledge is a seamless unity. Its guardians—Yukichi's father, our own ancestors, Mitiswangi—they're all blood brothers. This is a big thing to discover, an even bigger thing to take seriously. I think maybe you're better off without Yukichi, for now at least."

Turning back toward our hosts, I raised my gourd. "*Ihaichne,* we shall not forget you. You have made us happy. May the spirits be your friends—the spirits of the tapir, the woolly monkey, the jaguar, the piracucu, the toucan. May your medicine be strong, may you live long, may your children live long, may your manioc be fruitful, may your enemies be few, may peace stay with you."

We drank and danced, the children pulling Lotte back and forth, but she seemed far away, as if in some sort of trance of her own. Finally everyone drifted off to their hammocks and she remained by herself, staring quietly into the last embers of the fire. Sensing that she shouldn't be alone, I sat quietly in the shadows near her and waited. Minutes passed, then she began to talk, so quietly that I had to creep near her to make out the words.

> I was a lonely child. We lived in a little farming town where people were so proud of their land, my parents too. Everyone talked about the value of the land. Everyone went to church and asked God to protect the land and the harvests, as if the rest of the world, the world of technology and business, and even of books, was like the sea, held back by the dikes that might break and drown us. But I loved books and science and technology so much that sometimes I felt like I was the enemy, and I felt like people looked at me that way. Do you know what it's like to grow up in a town where intellectuals are called "space aliens," where the very word is linked with Molotov cocktails and armpit hair?
>
> When I was in high school there was this one boy I sort of liked, Jens. He could play the guitar and sing a little like Elvis Presley. He didn't laugh when I talked about archaeology or

penguins. One day I finally worked up the courage to tell him I wanted to go to college, and he just looked at me and said, "Why? Don't you think the guys here are good enough for you?" I didn't say it, but the answer was no, they bored the shit out of me, with their talk about Michael Jackson and alfalfa seed.

At first I really loved the university in Amsterdam, there was so much to see and learn; but gradually I found out that I didn't really belong there, either. It was a burlesque opposite of my hometown; the rule was that everything had to be absolutely the newest, the latest. I'd get interested in all this stuff—hip-hop culture, then clean energy, then Moroccan food—and spend hours, you know, learning its history and shades of expression. But that was all irrelevant, you see; you just had to know the buzz words and the personalities. You had know what to like and where to buy it, until something newer came along. Then you were suddenly a nerd if you didn't make snide jokes about the older thing. I was completely miserable. I didn't know where I was going. I didn't want to talk to anybody, and even my books seemed to be making fun of my misery.

The crummy apartment where I lived was right next to this huge public housing complex. I had to walk through it to get to my classes, and I could always smell Middle Eastern food and hear kids yelling in Arabic or Indonesian. There was this Turkish guy who worked in the market named Devrim, and I liked talking to him. He used to say things like, "Every human soul is tribal. It doesn't matter if you live in a metropolis like this, or alone in the middle of the desert, or in prison; your soul lives in a tribal village, where everyone knows everyone, for better or for worse." It turned out he was a puppeteer, performing in a tiny theater in the Turkish ghetto, where they put on the ancient shadow puppet plays called Karagoz. I started going to watch the plays. I couldn't understand the jokes, but they were coarse and simple comedies, and I imagined that I could follow the plots. They were the only thing that made me laugh or made me cry.

I was in love with Devrim. I stopped going to class and

asked him to teach me Turkish and show me everything about Karagoz, the characters and their traits, the meaning of the costumes and the jokes, how to make the gestures with the puppets, how this all fit into Turkish culture and history. I became completely absorbed. The traditional plays are divided into short episodes, and the puppeteer can combine episodes in new ways to make different stories. As I learned this, I started to feel that my real life and the Karagoz were changing places; that what happened to me at school or at home were really episodes drawn from the repertoire of a puppet theater, while the actual shadow puppets were real people. Ridiculous, I know, melodramatic, like that old film, *Lili*.

Well, that was fine, until one day Devrim told me he was going back to Turkey. I couldn't take it. I begged him to take me with him; I threatened to kill myself. One night during a performance I stood up in the audience and began to scream at his characters; I don't remember what I said—that they were killing me, that I was going to call the police, something like that. The children in the audience started crying, and their mothers took them away. Devrim came out into the empty theater and sat next to me while I cried. When I calmed down he asked me to come backstage. He handed me the puppet Nigár, the dancing woman, and said, "We are going to make a play. This is you." With Devrim playing the other parts, we made a play about our lives.

As the play unfolded, each scene creating the next one, I felt that I was no longer Lotte, I was Nigár. We went on and on. I was exhausted, I wanted to stop, but the other characters wouldn't let me, they kept urging me on and on, until I started to feel crazy, and I screamed, "No, no! I can't do it anymore!" but they said, "You have to! The play isn't over yet!" All of a sudden, something came up from inside me, and I felt calm. I realized that I was both Nigár and Lotte, and that we were every woman who had ever lived or ever would live; that what was happening to me had happened a million times and would

> go on forever—I could see it, I could hear it, I was very high up above the earth, watching it like a film, and I felt free.
>
> Before Devrim left, I knew what I wanted to do; to understand this unity that ran through us, Nigár, and me, and every woman. I dove into women's studies and philosophy and cultural anthropology, and they all kept pointing me backward, toward the past. I charged into history, then prehistory and archaeology, and finally into evolution, looking for the fundamental patterns. Before I knew it, I was in London, working on a PhD in integrative biology. And there it was; the interrelatedness of lives. Nigár and Lotte were products of communities, just as Devrim had said; each cell lives in circles like itself, each shaping the other, and those circles make up the tissues of wider circles, and those of wider still, until you come to communities of beings reaching up out of histories toward futures that are already carried in the memories of their DNA, already told in their puppet theaters.

I could hardly see her face in the failing light from the embers, but she turned and seemed to look at me for a moment. "What you said about the Web site of timelessness, I've seen it. Of course it's here, too. I knew that, but I forgot that each of us can only reach it with his own password."

"It's everywhere. The password is remembered in places like this, and in Karagoz theaters."

"And now I'm leaving."

"At one level, yes, at another level, no."

We stood. She stepped forward and held me for a moment, then turned and went to her hut. I was sure my pulse was making the roof shake. Triumph stood next to me, his trumpet at the ready. Why is it always too soon for him, I thought, but not for his cringing sister, doubt?

Chapter Twelve

The Two

On the two-day boat trip back down the Marañón and then the Amazon, Parkbourne spent most of the time on his computer. It was the first time I had seen him take notes, and I was itching to know what he was writing. Half of me wanted to engage him, to speak to him simply as a fellow human being, setting aside whatever had passed between us; my other half was tired of this whole thing and hoped he kept his distance. At times I looked out over the river and wondered what effect this tour would have on our little agency; at times I watched Lotte, tense and absorbed, downloading and editing her films and photographs.

We reached Iquitos in the late afternoon, numbed not just with the weariness of long discomfort and sensory overload, but from what I call re-entry shock. After weeks in the jungle you look around the human scene you left and realize with a kind of horror that you have landed on an unfamiliar planet—that the person you now are has never been here and doesn't know what to make of it. Parkbourne invited me to dine with them but I wanted passionately to be alone, and I said no. Lotte seemed distant and preoccupied. We arranged to meet at the agency the next day to finalize things; then climbed into separate taxis.

My phone woke me from a sound sleep about ten in the evening—the hour when a tropical town comes to life. I knew immediately it was Lotte. We met at the San Bruno, a small café near her hotel, over a pitcher of sangría. "I feel so lost, Morse, so unhappy. Does this happen to all your clients?"

"You're the first, except maybe for Yukichi."

"I googled 'environmental rights' this evening. I knew about most of it already, the stuff about the habitat, the resources, the sacred places. I always thought of native peoples as the proper guardians of what *we* value—natural beauty, diversity, wildness. I always thought of people like the Kurudahé as kind of ready-made park rangers; people who know what we need to know about the wild, people we could recruit to help us reach our own dreams. I never realized how…how narrow-minded, how self-centered that was. I never put it together with what you said about unity, about the integrity of a whole way of life, and how fragile that is."

"You must have known this at some level. I'm not that persuasive."

"It was you who explained it to me, but it was really Yukichi who showed me. Modernity broke his culture and in the process broke his life. Getting close to that vital, unbroken culture up there on the Marañón brought it home to him."

Her color began to heighten, her voice rose. "Of course, I saw how native people lived in the slums of Bogotá and Lima and Bangkok. I've seen the little Quechua whores here in Iquitos. I know how demoralizing it is for people to lose their way of life, but I always saw it as an economic suffering." She took a long drink and shook her head. "I thought if people could stay on their land, they could have the best of all worlds—their freedom, their traditions, and our economy. How can anyone possibly be so naïve?"

"Most people are, if they think about it at all."

"But you were not. Why? Please, tell me what happened to you, Morse. Please. It's so important to me to understand now."

I drained my glass and stood up. "Let's walk." The downtown streets were crowded, and we turned toward the quieter residential lanes. As we walked and walked I told her the entire story; about the *domhain comharthai* and the Conklin and the *fomors;* about the flashbacks. "As I look back now, it seems as though the last twenty years has been the unfolding of an unconscious plan. First my choice of psychology as a profession, then the growth of my interest in shamanism, my apprenticeships with healers. I already knew quite a bit about the lore of the Amazonian people before I came here."

"Have you met anyone else who understands this?"

I shook my head. "Years ago I spent a few days in a locked psychiatric ward. I wasn't crazy, of course. I only made the mistake of, shall we say, sharing my private thoughts. Maybe that's why I'm so comfortable with the Kurudahé. We don't talk about it, but I know that if we did, they'd understand perfectly. They're like brothers to me."

The streets were almost empty now. We had come to a little park at the side of an old church whose flaking plaster wall was floodlit. A few small iguanas scurried among the bushes, and we stopped and gazed up at a huge banyan tree, the home of an active tribe of titi, and she turned to me. "It must hurt so to talk about it; so much loneliness. But it's beautiful, beautiful."

For a second I doubted that she had understood a word I had said. How was it possible that another human being would find my odyssey beautiful—let alone a vital, exciting woman? She was looking at the church, but I could tell by her eyes that she knew what I was feeling, and then I knew that she *had* understood, and I had to lean down and kiss her so she couldn't see my tears; my God, there were so many of them. It was a short kiss, but it made us both tremble, and the second one was the long one. We hurried back to my place awkwardly holding hands, and in bed we were so urgent, like two drowning people. All night we kept waking up and giving in to the hunger, letting it rise up and overwhelm us. I woke up exhausted at first light, and as I lay watching her sleep, I began to cry again.

I use my spear to balance as I climb down the last tier of boulders, but it's slow and painful. A few yards farther down I see where the path crosses a meadow alongside a rushing stream, then enters a birch forest at the distance of a hawk's cry. When I finally reach the meadow I set my heavy burden down to catch my breath. For two days now I've been carrying this great block of ice that I cut from the edge of the glacier high up Gur Mountain. It's as heavy as the body of a stag. I can't rest long; it's three or more days' journey to the River Thurn, where I must build a raft to take my burden to our village on the other side.

Halfway to the woods, I hear human voices and crouch for cover in the grass, creeping forward to get a look. As I draw nearer, I can make out the words, a southern dialect of my language. It could be the same group I passed on the way up, who gave me a few strips of dried deer meat and let me rest by their fire. It could also be one of the outcast bandit troops that haunt the trading route through the pass, but if that's the case they'll probably pick up my trail and follow me anyway and find I carry nothing of value. I stand and walk toward them.

They have set up a skin lean-to on the bank, where two old women are working, one plaiting a basket from birch bark strips, the other scraping the fat from a deer hide. A couple of toddlers run to hide behind them as I approach. Some younger men and women are in the river, carrying stones and setting stakes to build a fish trap. They have made a game out of it; the squealing women and youths trying to trip the men as they stagger under the weight of the rocks; the roaring men trying to catch them and dunk their heads. As I approach a little way downstream they stop to look at me; then realize it was I who passed here several days ago, and go back to their game. It's fun to watch. I set my ice load down again and plant the haft of my spear in the soft earth by the water so that I can kneel and drink. I sense something and look up to see one of the young women staring at me. Her neck is unusually long. Tangles of dark wet hair frame an olive-skinned face with large white teeth. She looks away, but not before I feel a silent cry go out, the cry of pleasure you can hear only in your heart. I turn my eyes from her, and I feel the cry continue.

With the stone point of my spear I cut a reed from the bank, and in a few minutes I've fashioned it into a simple flute. A few of the young people come over and listen to me, but she only watches from a distance. After a while I take up my pack and spear again and move slowly downstream to a place where the trees reach the water's edge. I sit on a stone among the trees and continue to play my flute.

Soon I see her a little way off, pretending to gather firewood. I stand and move toward her slowly, blowing soft low notes. She is smiling shyly, holding an armload of small branches. I pick up a branch from the ground and draw close, holding it out to her. Her breast is heaving. Her hand trembles as she reaches for my branch, and her bundle falls clattering to the ground. We both stoop to gather it up, and our heads are only a hand span apart. She's whimpering with distress and excitement, and I'm trembling too. I can smell her body and her wet hair. I hand her the sticks and sit cross legged, as she stands and moves back a step. I point to myself. "Goric." I point to her.

"Te'ana," she says. "Where?" pointing up toward the mountain.

"Gur. I have ice," pointing to my pack, I motion her to come. She hesitates, but curiosity is pulling her, and she comes.

With words and pantomime I explain: "In my tribe, a man must cut his own land from the forest before he can marry. First, he must prove his manhood. He must go to the top of Gur, bring back ice. The ice stays in the men's lodge. Sick people are cured by it. When the ice has melted, the man must stop cutting his land. He must never cut more. You understand?"

"If he doesn't bring the ice?"

"He may never marry. He becomes a witch, unless he is killed in war."

"Who will you marry?"

"I don't know." If I had said this before I saw her, it would have been a lie, but now it is true. "Do you have a husband?"

She doesn't answer. Her eyes are desperate and full of longing. I touch her face, begin caressing her cheek, her ear, her mouth, and in a little while she starts to relax, her eyes listening to my mind, saying, Yes to this, yes to that, yes to everything. Something is happening in my chest and arms and legs, not like fire, but stretched, like something was swelling inside me. It makes me imagine every possible male thing, and her eyes keep listening and saying yes, yes. I touch her hand and she takes hold of mine, fiercely.

"I will stay here," I say; but she shakes her head, her eyes wild

again. "Then come with me." We stand, our hands still locked together. "Now," I say. "Soon the darkness will begin." I pick up my pack of ice and my spear. She puts her arms around me tightly, like an excited child, and every place we touch feels like a hungry mouth. Now we're walking together, not thinking about anything except the taste of that.

We hear voices far behind us, and we begin to walk faster, but I can't keep up the pace because of the ice. I drop the ice in the woods, and we begin to run.

As always, the overwhelming realism of the flashback left me shaken, confused. I wondered if Lotte had been watching me but saw that she was still peacefully asleep. I lay back and breathed deeply, trying to calm myself, to understand what had just happened. The earlier flashbacks had all been triggered by anger, fear, hatred, lust; this one was obviously different. What were the *fomors* up to this time? I began to calm down, and I looked at Lotte again, and it hit me:

This wordless transformation, this discovery of an unsuspected self through the simple proximity of another, was part of the *domhain comharthai* as well, one of the eternal fundamentals of human nature, unchanged since the darkest past. In a moment, the meaning and value of everything can be canceled, the script can be erased, time can begin again at zero. Everything I had experienced, through endless incarnations, and re-experienced in my flashbacks, and fought for, and fought against, and longed for, was nothing in the face of love. The words of Dryr, the *fomor* I'd met on the *sidh* of Cuimhne, came back to me: "We *fomors* don't ask *why,*" Dryr had said, calling it the question of a weakling. Being immortal themselves, the *fomors* can feel anger and even fear—the fear of anonymity—but not compassion. *Why* is the question of understanding, of compassion. Love, compassion, is the one great thing that makes the gods of light infinitely wiser and more powerful. Love makes them sensitive to death, a sensitivity that alone leads to insight and understanding.

As if nudged by my thoughts, Lotte opened her eyes.

"I'll come with you," I said. We lay there looking at each other, drinking this moment, getting drunk on it. "The flashbacks I told you about last night, I just had another one while you were sleeping."

"Oh, no!"

"Wait. This one was completely different. Thousands of years ago I fell in love, the exact feeling I have for you right now, and in a moment I gave up my whole life, my whole future, to be with her. You see? The person, the single consciousness, is not the center. The deep code has no center. The person doesn't exist, except as a passing thought, a momentary expression of the code, and the code now makes us into the expression of love."

"What happens now?"

"The code decides everything."

"I don't like it!"

"The code has always decided everything; for example, that we should meet, that we should fall in love. Can you feel it? That we are being born right now, miraculously, unique and original, in a brand new universe that was impossibly created just now, just for this?"

The confusion on her face slowly melted. We began to laugh and cry, and we opened as wide as history and dove into the abyss of each other, fell off this universe into another one in which this moment made sense of everything.

It was nine o'clock when she finally called Parkbourne and apologized, telling him we would meet him at Jaime's office. "Everything's fine," she said. She hung up and crawled into my arms again for a long minute, then said, "You have to stay here, lover. Shit, I don't want to go without you, but you're needed here, you know. I'll come back soon. You know I will, don't you?"

"Of course I believe you, but—"

She stopped me with a kiss. "New York would kill you, kill us. We can e-mail every day, ten times a day, until I wind things up. A few weeks, okay? We are the code."

"The code is us."

Chapter Thirteen

The Recording

In just eleven weeks we were together again in Iquitos. For the next week we got out of bed only for urgent bodily needs; and for ten days after that we wandered the shops, parks, and restaurants mindlessly, drunk on the novelty of our bond, lost in the exploration of the vast new territories each life presented to the other; mapping the vineyards of our tastes, the twisting trails of our travel and reading, the wide waters of our dreams, the thickets of our hurt. For hours I would watch her fingers imperfectly caress Villa-Lobos, Corelli, Bach from her guitar. I would make her laugh doing George Carlin or Richard Pryor.

At last the morning did come when we woke and began to wonder what our endless unread e-mails held, and within hours we were back in the wide world. While in New York, Lotte had hoped to learn the fund's plans for the Marañón Basin, so that we could plan a counterstrategy; but this hadn't been possible. A cloud of suspicion hung over her expedition, thanks to Yukichi's defection and the fact that she couldn't completely conceal her relationship with me, and she had found herself increasingly isolated at the fund. The best she could do was to read the official reports and listen to the office gossip to decipher their meaning.

"Shit!" she yelled from the kitchen, and coming in I found her sitting on the counter in a white dressing gown, her laptop on her crossed legs. The image made me laugh.

"A cursing Buddha. Does enlightenment elude you?"

"All you get about Peru on the Fund's fucking Web site are official reports full of boring talk about projects to 'improve the sustainable development of natural resources,' and 'bring indigenous communities into the orbit of civil authority.' This budget here, it has a huge item for 'transportation improvements in the Amazon,' but it doesn't tell you where the hell it is, or what the hell they're improving. Look. This page talks about 'cultural barriers to development.' We know what that means, don't we? 'Enlightening' the local people on the joys of the world monoculture."

"The blessing that kills. But time is on our side, love. The ancient wisdom will prevail. Remember my last flashback? Creation and destruction are the surface of the Deep Code; the basic energy, the seamless knowledge, goes on unchanged forever."

"Hmph. I liked you better as an angry young man. You're not going off in the woods to contemplate your navel, are you, speaking of Buddhas?"

"The fire's still there, as much as ever. It's only lost its bitterness, that's all. The first lesson I learned from the *fomors* was that I, and everyone around me, was living a pompous illusion. The second lesson was that it doesn't matter. You know Carl Jung's psychology, I'm sure."

"The great interpreter of dreams…"

"Carved over the doorway of Jung's house in Basel was an inscription from the temple of the Delphic Oracle: 'Summoned or not, God will be there.'"

"Should we not fight, then? And don't give me that pious shit, like 'Living right is the same as fighting.' It's not, in my book."

"There are a lot of ways to fight, Lotte. At any given moment, who knows which is the best?"

"And what is *our* way?"

"I don't know, but I can tell you what it's not. It's not trying to squeeze sensitive information out of the frigging World Development Fund while sitting in the frigging jungle, ten thousand miles away."

"Smartass," she frowned and slowly closed the laptop.

She came with me on the next tour. I had already been back to the Kurudahé and found Yukichi thriving, making friends with nearby tribes and learning their dialects with amazing speed. A stranger could easily mistake him for a native now; even his posture, gestures, and facial expressions blended in. He was pleased to see Lotte's happiness, but her presence also troubled him. "When will we see bulldozers?" he wondered, sitting cross-legged in the tribal lodge while the children climbed over him. We shook our heads and agreed we should enjoy the way things were for the time being.

Masanch stayed on as our traveling companion, and things were almost ideal for the four of us. Our ties were increasingly with the jungle and with each other. With each expedition, Lotte's understanding of the biota was deepening; and thanks to Yukichi and Masanch, our knowledge of the people was too. As the months went by, our little company began to attract a new kind of visitor; not just the naturalist with a rain forest project, but the specialist—the scholar, the artist with a focused interest in this particular niche of the natural world. Our guests wanted to stay in the jungle for weeks or months, learn the Kurudahé language, apply the lessons of this unique ecosystem in new ways. Our trips to Iquitos shrank in frequency and duration. In the city we found ourselves toying with our chicken or steak and dreaming about toucan and monkey. Even our bodies changed, as the strenuous life and low-fat diet reshaped us into sinewy animals. When our computer broke down we put off buying a new one, and one day realized we no longer needed more than notebooks and pencils. The preoccupations of the media seemed less and less important, and we rarely watched television or read the news when we were in town. Hardly anyone but Jaime ever phoned me, so we spent our rare days in the city writing letters by hand to faraway friends and family.

As for the Deep Code—meaning both the *domhain comharthai* and the Kurudahé spirits—I no longer had flashbacks. Lotte asked if she could be introduced to *natem*, and Mitiswangi agreed. Maybe because she was a biologist, the visions and sensations of snakes didn't frighten her, even at first; and after a few sessions it seemed as if she was conversing with the spirits more easily than the rest of us. We would sit by the river in the evening with some of the men and talk about the meaning of what we had seen on our *natem* journeys. When we began to hunt with them too, they were content to have her along. Her hand with the blowgun was unsteady, but her spirit songs seemed to improve our success.

The dry season had come again. Lotte and I had just come back to Iquitos after a month up the river with a group of environmentalists from Oregon. It was lucky we came back when we did, because one of our clients, a tiny grandmother named Hester, was a veterinarian, and Ruby the anaconda happened to be suffering from acute constipation. Hester prescribed daily hot baths for Ruby for the time being and actually agreed to stay in town to see how things went. Jaime, beside himself with gratitude, cut Hester's fare in half and passed around a bottle of good Ecuadorian rum.

As we sipped and discussed the trip, my attention was caught by a note on Jaime's desk with an unusual name on it. "Who is Pulin Naray?" I asked.

"Oh! I almost forgot," he said. "This Señor Naray called a couple of weeks ago. Asked for you. Seemed upset that you weren't here."

"About booking a tour?"

"Apparently not. Didn't say what he wanted. Wouldn't talk to anyone else." He handed me the note, and I saw the name and phone number of the Hotel Maldonado. I called. Yes, Señor Naray was still among the guests. No, he wasn't in just now. I left my number and we went to dinner.

When Naray called that night about eleven, I learned that he was a freelance journalist and, by his accent, a native of India. He didn't want to discuss his business on the phone but asked if he could come to my apartment right away. Half an hour later, a chubby middle-aged man appeared, wearing a rumpled linen suit and carrying a battered laptop and digital audio recorder in a handwoven shoulder bag featuring the pyramids at Giza. His gaze was steady, and I couldn't keep my eyes from his, with their dark circles and their haunted look.

"Is there anyone else here?" he asked in a low voice after greeting us and taking a seat. I assured him there was not. "I'm working on the story of Mister Richard Parkbourne's death," he said.

"Parkbourne is dead!?" We both spoke at once.

"I see," he said. The looks on our faces clearly embarrassed him. "I'm sorry to be the one who brings you sad news. I thought you might have been in contact with him, you see." He leaned back and stared at the ceiling. "This complicates things, but of course it's not your fault."

"Can you tell us about it?" Lotte said, still shaken.

"Of course. I'm sorry." He was studying us closely now. "His plane crashed in the Philippine Sea, with four people on board, almost two months ago now. Few details are available. The official word is, either mechanical failure or pilot error."

"But you don't believe that," she said.

"Such a prominent person, of course there are always lots of questions."

"And you came here hoping we had some answers?" she asked.

"Anything you know about him would be helpful."

"I'm sorry to ask this, Mr. Naray, but can you show us something—" I began.

"To authenticate my identity? You're quite welcome." From his coat pocket he produced his passport, then he opened his laptop, tapped in a few commands, and brought up an article he had written on the plane crash. It was from the *New York Times,* dated two months earlier. It all looked quite legitimate.

While Lotte made tea, Naray told us a little of his background as an investigative reporter. His stories had led to the conviction of a Serbian dictator and a Chicago slumlord, the closing of a Chinese chemical plant, and the cancellation of an Indian dam project. We talked about Parkbourne until three in the morning, about Lotte's work at the World Development Fund and her recruitment for the Amazon project, and about our trip up the Marañón.

When we came to the story of the *natem* session, Naray asked if he could record the discussion. From his shoulder bag he took a battered digital voice recorder, patched here and there with silver duct tape. He switched it on, tested it, and began asking for fine details. What is the *natem* experience like? Why did he take it? What did he do while intoxicated? What did he say about it? Who else was there? Did his behavior change afterward? Did he mention any similar experiences he'd had? Did we have any conversations with him about Kurudahé belief, or about spirit travel in general?

"Mister Naray," I said finally, "Quite of a few of our clients have taken *natem.* Some find it enlightening, others are confused, still others say nothing at all. We never talked about intimate things with Parkbourne; we really have no idea how he took the experience. We couldn't see any obvious change in him. He must have been affected by Yukichi's defection at least, but even there, he was not the sort of man who showed his feelings."

"Just the opposite, in fact," Lotte said. "Do you have reason to think he was affected more than we know?"

Naray turned off his recorder, stood, and began to pace the room, arms folded, head down. He stopped and looked at us. "You haven't been following the news about the Fund, you say. You wouldn't know abut the changes he was starting to make there, the uproar in the global trade community. Soon after he came back from the Amazon, he ordered a complete environmental impact review of their ongoing projects and plans. He called for the creation of a Division of Cultural Preservation; he was bringing in anthropologists, requiring contract language on indigenous rights. What really drove the global traders crazy was his call last November for a Fund-led conference of fair trade organizations. Some board members thought he had lost his mind, started to talk about firing him; but he had powerful allies in the green movement pushing back."

Holy shit, I thought. They wanted him dead. "Do you think his *natem* experience could have been behind all this?" I asked.

"I don't know what to think. He made a recording of a phone conversation a few weeks before he died. I have it. I don't know who has heard it, but the media apparently have not. Based on our discussion tonight, I want to play it for you."

By now it was already light outside and we were all hungry, but there was little in the apartment to eat. The three of us pushed through the downtown morning crowds to the Café San Bruno on a side street off the hotel district. We picked a table in the back and ordered coffee, eggs, and *pan dulce.* Naray pulled his laptop from the Egyptian shoulder bag, opened it, and clicked on an audio file. The sound quality was poor, but we immediately recognized Parkbourne's bland, self-confident manner of speaking. The recording began somewhere in the middle of the conversation. The other voice had a pronounced accent that sounded vaguely Southeast Asian to me. After a couple of sentences Naray clicked PAUSE. "I'm not sure who the other voice is," he said. "See if you have any ideas." He hit PLAY again.

Parkbourne: I'm sorry, I didn't hear all of that. Could you—

Other voice: I said, these new requirements are encouraging the enemies of the Fund. You must know that.

P: Which requirements? You mean giving local satraps the shiny new advisor badges?

O: That, and this thing about environmental law enforcement, all that stuff.

P: That's one kind of lens to use. Look through another lens and you could say we're making boon companions of the opposition.

O: How can we do that? They reject our entire philosophy of development. If we keep making concessions, they will just—

P: Crank up the heat? Get a tailor who works in asbestos. Look, what did our audit show? Most of our project districts are nourishing thieves' markets and bordellos, empty schools, and soaring rotgut rum sales. The cultural rights gurus might know something we don't.

O: What are you suggesting? That we consult them in the planning process?

P: (laughing) My friend, if anyone in this game can be called educated, broad from ear to ear, and solid as brass, it's you. Orthodox thinking says that the world will soon be Shangri-la if we just stick with the mainstream economists; that we'd be having a regular epidemic of happiness if it weren't for the anarchist tree-huggers. Is that the real picture? Or might there be forms of intelligence, real save-the-ship knowledge, right there where we're aiming the tear gas? Don't you sometimes wonder if we're steaming in a circle? I know you do.

O: Of course, but scuttling the ship won't help. You sound like a socialist! What do you mean by "forms of intelligence"?

P: You know I like to get the mud of our projects between my toes. I've been all over hell, spoken with the local people, supped and snored and sambaed with them. They didn't learn how to skin a goat from us, or how to be happy doing it—

O: So let's make them Directors?! Do we have time for this discussion?

P: Ah, yes. Quite right. Time is the realm of the coin. The people whose needs we claim to serve have spent millennia learning the language of their land, an impossible waste of centuries, but the miracle is, their children know the basics by the time they're five. By the time they're twenty-five, some can see past the barriers of time we consider fixed, can understand relationships our science has yet to grasp.

O: (pause) Richard, I thought the talk about replacing you was a bit hysterical, but I'm beginning to see where it comes from. You may have powerful friends in the green movement, even in governments of the global south, but you're not invincible, not if you keep this up.

P: Thanks for your honesty. I've always respected you for that. I'll see you at the council on Thursday, then.

O: I can't make it. You'll see my COO, Sawanipat. Good-bye, Richard.

P: Good-bye.

"What do you make of it?" Naray asked.

Lotte and I had been reading each other's eyes, and we sat silent, breathing heavily.

"This is the only sample I have of these ideas of his," Naray went on. "He must have deeply trusted the person. Yes, I'm pretty sure they killed him. You have no idea whom he was talking to?" We shook our heads.

"Who? Who killed him?" Lotte asked.

"The suspects are many, many. The traditions of the World Development Fund kept enormous structures of power and wealth in place. It was the power behind a score of thrones, the stamp of approval on hundreds of high appointments, the guarantor of billions in corporate wealth. He must have known the risk he was taking."

"What happened to him here in the Amazon might well have

triggered such a change in his thinking," I said. "Going back to his *natem* experience—I've spent years studying shamanism, what you might call the Deep Code, or the art of soul travel. I know from experience how profoundly a sensitive mind can be affected by a glimpse of this knowledge. It certainly changed my life."

"And mine," Lotte said.

He switched on his recorder. "Tell me about it," He said. Lotte gripped my hand. "Off the record," he added.

"The knowledge is all there," I began, "in the writings of ethnology, folklore, psychology. What's needed, to make it real and personal, is a living experience that breaches our fear of the unknown..." As I talked—of the basic tenets of shamanism, of New Guinea's Raapa Uu, of the Navajo, the West African Yoruba, the Druids, the Kurudahé—something began to uncoil in my mind, something bigger and more unsettling than the snake visions of *natem*: The *fomors* had become bankers, they now knew intimately the world in which Parkbourne moved. The world of finance had become their domain, the *sidh* where they threw out and gathered in their cunning nets. Had he offended them, or fallen into one of their deadly fairy tales? I remembered Dryr's fury at the thought of the Celtic heroes. Parkbourne was the modern equivalent of those heroes; were they bent on protecting their power from such a challenge? They saw the future; they arranged it. They knew very well that Parkbourne was bent on using the very power that they so jealously guarded to destroy their modern temples of worship.

But wait.

The *fomors* were not the sole owners of the Deep Code. The gods of light and life, Dagdá and Danán and the other good Druids, the guardian spirits of the Kurudahé and their neighbors, the healing wind voices of the world's shamans, all of them shared that plane of existence where all time is here, now.

What was the timeless meaning of Parkbourne's death? Suppose the world at large should learn the story. A brilliant and powerful man, a man with his fingers on the global economy's levers of control, goes to the Amazon jungle, drinks a mind-expanding potion with the native people, and comes back with ancient knowledge, knowledge that might restore something immeasurably precious from a world that modernity is bent on erasing. But the guardians of modernity (human? supernatural?) discover this, and they murder him. It was so familiar, facile. The great legend cycle of the Hero Thief—Prometheus, Sisyphus, Isaiah, Robin Hood. But this time it was not a legend; it was real, and it carried a powerful message for humankind—Saint Joan, Galileo, Gandhi. And what if this story should be revealed, in all its amazing detail, throughout the stricken world, the world of broken cultures and cardboard cities and polluted streams and hunger wages? This too could have been the plan, the history that had already been written in the Deep Code.

Naray listened quietly as I spoke, of the *domhain comharthai,* the plane of knowledge outside time, of the Kurudahé spirits residing at a level that is pure essence, above the chaotic stream of lived experience. "Where did we go wrong? With the creation of writing and print? Those great vehicles of civilization have simply run over the ancient wisdom, crushed it. You see, it can't be captured and tamed in language. It's nonlinear, it begins where language leaves off. It must be transmitted directly from the matrix of the Deep Code to the individual mind. Writing, by codifying and propagating so-called knowledge at the level of language, creates orthodoxies of dead belief: religion as we know it; science."

I had been watching his face carefully and could read nothing there but concentrated attention. "You believe," he said, "that Parkbourne had discovered, had been exposed to this...this Deep Code, and that he meant to apply it to a new kind of economics?"

"Possibly."

"With what effect?"

"I'm not sure. Maybe with the effect of restoring *local* knowledge, intimate knowledge of familiar places and people, to the core of human endeavor."

"What would that look like?"

"Again, I don't know. An economics that preserves relationships at the expense of material things? An infinitely diverse human world, where the customs of actual ancestors take precedence over such deadly abstractions as 'efficiency,' and 'progress'? Enlightened institutions protecting against the loss of cherished meaning and value?"

"How could this ever be accomplished?"

"Maybe it couldn't. But if the guardians of local knowledge, the shamans and artists and storytellers, were given a seat at the table as Parkbourne seems to be saying there—"

Naray switched off his recorder and we sat silently for a minute before we rose. "This is something I have to work on," he said. "It gives new potential meaning to all my notes. Give me a couple of days, and I'll call you again."

"We might never know *who* killed him," Lotte said, "but if the world knew *why,* his death might turn out to be worth something." We shook hands with him and watched him hurry off down the street, which had fallen quiet in the scorching midday sun.

At home we lay in our hammocks on the open veranda, talking little. "I think Naray understands what we talked about," she said. "If he does, I wonder what he'll do. Do you think he'll write the truth, try to get the true story into the media?"

"If he does, is he likely to succeed?" I wondered. Between us, we knew almost nothing of the world of journalism. I fell asleep feeling helpless and confused.

The next morning, Saturday, we heard spasmodic downpours punctuated by the splattering sounds of gushing gutters under a sudden searing sun. As soon as we were awake, Lotte and I independently had the same thought. "Let's go to the news shop by the cathedral and buy some papers," she said.

"And magazines. And maybe we should get the computer fixed." We ate a quick breakfast, took our umbrellas, and walked the half mile to the news shop on Plaza Grau. We bought the London *Times, El Tiempo,* and *Newsweek.* We were near the Hotel Maldonado, and Lotte suggested that we drop in on Naray.

An ambulance and two squad cars sat in the street in front of the hotel, their flashing lights reflected in the wet street. People entering and leaving the hotel were being stopped and questioned. As we stood there wondering what to do, two ambulance attendants came out pushing a gurney that clearly bore a body covered by a black tarp. Behind them came two uniformed officers, one carrying a battered leather suitcase and Naray's Egyptian shoulder bag. The other carried a clear plastic folder, within which I recognized the remains of Naray's voice recorder. It looked as if it had been flattened with a sledge hammer.

Knees shaking, we turned and walked back toward Plaza Grau, trying not to hurry or to look around. Lotte was sobbing quietly. "We've got to leave Iquitos, today," I said.

She nodded. "To the jungle."

"No. Too risky for all of us. The Kurudahé are identified."

"Pucallpa?"

I shook my head. "Nowhere nearby. It would be best to get out of Peru, but they're likely to be watching."

That day we packed what we could carry and went to the Belen District to find Masanch. Without speaking to anyone, the three of us then stole one of Jaime's motor canoes and made for the upper reaches of the Marañón. With his uncanny knowledge of the river, Masanch continued at the helm, navigating by moonlight and by ear long after dark, then motored up a small tributary to land, so that our canoe could not be seen from the river. Along the way I turned the whole story over in my mind, trying to decide whether or not we had gotten it right, and if so, how to explain it to others. It was especially important to make it clear to Masanch, because of his involvement. Parkbourne's killers would have to assume that he knew the story too. Back in Iquitos I had only told him that Parkbourne was killed because he knew things that could destroy some powerful people, and that we had to run because we knew this. That, he understood at once.

When we had made camp I sat next to him in front of the fire. "I have to explain to you why this has happened," I began. "Señor Parkbourne was a powerful person, almost as powerful as the head of the national government. He was able to tell many, many people what to do, and to give them the money to do it."

"He had the manner of a *patrón*," Masanch nodded.

"A very great *patrón*. When he gave orders, the fortunes of many people were affected. Some of those people were very big *patrones* as well. They did what he said because they trusted him, they believed he was their ally.

"But you said he was not?"

"At first he was, for a long time. But when he came here to Amazonas, he learned some new things that changed his way of thinking. Before, he thought that he was helping the whole world when he helped his allies. He thought he was making people all over the world happier. But after he came here, he saw that he had been wrong."

Masanch laughed. "No one has that kind of power, not even the *aroe.* Happiness is like this." He closed his eyes and held his hands over his heart.

"Yes. Well, when some people have become very big *patrones* for a very long time, they forget that; they think they can make people happy by making them more like *patrones*, by giving them the same kinds of things. When Señor Parkbourne realized this was wrong, he tried to convince his allies to stop."

He nodded. "But if they admitted they could not make people happy, then they would lose their power. Why did he tell them that?"

"After he came here, he realized that trying to make people live like *patrones* was not only useless, it was actually harmful. It made the *patrones* more powerful than ever, because everyone would then depend on them; but it destroyed the jungle, it confused the young people. He believed that he could show his allies a better way, a way of letting people find their own happiness, by respecting the way they are."

"But the *patrones* wanted to keep their power."

"This made him their enemy, and because we know this..." I drew my finger across my neck.

We were silent for a while, then Lotte said, "The knowledge of the Kurudahé, of all the jungle people, is something our white ancestors used to know, but we forgot it a long time ago. In many ways it is a far more powerful knowledge than what we were taught by our elders, and now the ability to see it is coming back everywhere, little by little. What happened to Señor Parkbourne is just an example. The *patrones* are frightened by it, they think they have to fight against it, but in the end they will lose and it will take its place everywhere again, maybe after we are gone."

"You will see this through the eyes of your grandchildren," Masanch said and put another stick on the fire. Lotte put her arm around his shoulder.

"Even as we see it now," I said.

It took us seventeen days to walk through the jungle from the river system into Ecuador, stopping to drink *natem* and share stories with the Jivaro, the Aguaruna, the Huambisa, the Achuar. Each place we stopped, we asked them if they knew that more and more foreigners would soon come here with huge machines to make roads and bring their powerful medicine and motorbikes and MP3s. All of them said yes, they knew that, and they knew that such things were nothing to admire; that such things begin by destroying the souls of people who want them, and once their souls are dead, the people end up destroying the forest itself. Then we told them that they had *ihaichne,* cousins, all over the vast world, who could also speak to the spirits of the plants and birds and fish, and that together, they and their *ihaichne* will some day save the world when they teach these things to the foreigners, so as to bring their dead souls back to life.

Chapter Fourteen

Guayaquil

So here I sit, in the district jail near Guayaquil, waiting. As hard as life is here, I am not in a hurry to get out. The longer they keep me here, the better it will be for our cause. It would be even better if they executed me, but I doubt they are stupid enough to do that. Lotte and I have spent three years gathering around us many who would instantly take my death as a call to battle, and they in turn have gathered many more who would follow them. These people understand deeply the mission of Otro Camino Arriba, and its epic importance. Both the battle-weary veterans whose quiet work keeps our agenda alive in the political and financial capitals of the western hemisphere, and the fiery young people who keep our cause in the news with their strident public voices. OCA helps to organize fair-trade networks, connecting indigenous farmers and craftspeople with brokers and outlets in the north. We gather and publish information on unfair trade and labor practices, land grabs, destruction of natural resources. We mobilize workers and students to lever public pressure for change. Sometimes our friends and supporters are recognized in the press; more often they are arrested, fined, or fired, far from the public eye, but this is what we, and they, expect.

These people and these struggles are our daily bread, our life's blood, for Lotte and me. We staff a kind of command post behind the front lines. Until I was arrested, we shared a tiny office in a shabby suite above a tire repair shop in Avenida Guarancal, but we were rarely there. Usually we worked at our home computers. We gathered and sent the steady stream of news, instructions, requests, encouragements, commiserations, alerts, alarms, manifestos that kept OCA alive. It has become a passion to all of us, as beautiful as it is stressful and dangerous. Lotte and I wanted to have children, but we worry about giving them a safe and comfortable home to grow up in. The indigenous people, the subsistence farmers, the urban squatters with whom we worked have become in a way our family. Lotte especially frets and laughs and grieves with them as only a sister or a mother or a daughter can, and there is no need to ask each other whether we are happy.

So what am I doing here in the Guayaquil provincial jail? The business of my arrest started three months ago. A year earlier, OCA had been chosen as the lead organization for the international human rights conference Voices of the Global South. More than eleven hundred people, three hundred and thirty-two organizations from fifty-three countries. Six months of madhouse activity had put the meetings in place—lodgings for the guests, meeting rooms, the program, the equipment, entertainment, press arrangements, logistics, staff, and volunteers, the whole thing.

Under the nervous eye of the local authorities the planes touched down in Guayaquil, the buses and cars roared in, the meeting rooms filled. Here a group of tall African figures in dashikis with British accents, there a circle of Quechua speakers in their bright wool ponchos and felt hats. Mayan villagers in their intricately embroidered skirts and blouses, mixed in among the tattooed faces of Maori chiefs. Women in saris and in burkas, bearded young men in turbans, grandmothers in sarongs, students of all colors laughing, strolling about with their cell phones glued to their ears. The purpose of the conference was to strengthen the movement for indigenous rights. We wanted to bring in new participants and to attract public attention, but we also knew that the chance for each of us to spend time with experienced and dedicated colleagues would re-ignite our desire, strengthen our confidence, deepen our commitment, refresh our spirits. But we were not prepared for what actually began to happen during the first days.

We wanted the point of view of indigenous people at the margins of modernity to be the keynote for the conference; and for the opening session a group of native healers from several tribes took the stage. Their styles and imagery accented the diversity of their lives and personalities. But at once it was also clear that their views were unified, like the pieces of an intricate puzzle, by a subtle theme, the very theme of this story. The so-called civilized people of the world are only beginning to understand, but for our indigenous colleagues all over the world there is a deep understanding and a way of life—the understanding that nature and the divine are one, and a way of living whereby every act expresses that unity.

Sitting in my bare cell I can easily call to my mind's eye every detail of the conference. Yosi, a shaman from highland New Guinea, spoke first. A small, wiry man, bent with age, he spoke without a microphone, in a high, piping voice, but in the quiet hall that voice seemed to come from everywhere at once. He spoke of his ancestors, the spirits of his forest, until their unfamiliar names surrounded us and drew us inward, like the exotic flowers of an otherworldly jungle. Through this jungle came, somehow—all of us could see his message in vivid colors—a plane of knowing where the living, the dead, and the unborn come together to teach the willing student. Few young people of his village want to learn the names now, he said, but if the names are lost, it will be as if human beings have lost their ears and will never again know the sounds of the forest.

The room was already electrified when Mitiswangi spoke, the healer from the village of Tukos, whom you already know well. Though old and lame now, he was a thunderbolt. He spoke not of ancestors or spirits, but of his training as a healer. Since the beginning of time, he said, the spirits have seen to it that certain people have the power to concentrate, to push their senses past the surface of things, past the eyes of the jaguar and the chameleon, past the bitterness of the manioc, past the blackness of the night, and past the illusion of time's footsteps. With self-discipline and the help of herbs, such people become like the soil where the seeds of knowledge are planted, to grow and produce new seeds for the next generation, on and on forever. The ancient stories are like water on this soil, and if the children don't hear them, again and again, then the soil of people's souls will become dry, and there will be no more healers.

A storyteller, a regally round, laughing presence of a woman named Hava, from Kauai, spoke of how the pieces of Polynesian knowing fit together—kinship, agriculture, music, navigation, worship, fishing, even war—each reinforcing and guiding the others, like the planks, mast, sails of a perfect canoe. The ancients knew this; knew that they had to keep building the canoe of all knowledge, and sailing it across time, back to the days of the myths, and forward onto the great sea of time, in search of the source of life itself. "This is why you are here," she smiled. "To build up the canoe. To teach the world how to build it up, the world that cannot sail and is afraid of the sea."

As the several voices gave the same message, a presence began to be felt in the auditorium, an awareness of something completely unexpected and almost frightening in strength. People looked at each other, some in astonishment, some with smiles of recognition. A page was being turned in the book of knowledge—or perhaps, thousands of pages, turned back to a place where the great forgetting we call civilization had begun. Or perhaps the book itself was dissolving into another medium, a single perfect canoe, a timeless medium of relationships, where the voices from the henge stones and the drum circles could be heard again by us and by the shamans still in out there in the womb of all life. We looked at ourselves through the eyes of these people, our living ancestors, and saw how little and how poor we had become. It was not just brain knowledge, not just the effect of a stirring lecture, something to be discussed over drinks and scribbled in our notebooks. It was the voice that had been calling us forward all along, made suddenly more clear. We walked out into the fading Guayaquil dusk in twos and threes, knowing that something large had been born, and this large thing would be in all of us wherever we went from now on.

On Saturday, the second day of the conference, I sat at the OCA info desk in the lobby of the main lecture hall. Lotte was across town, at the office, minding the phones, and she called me on my cell with terrible news from Cruzita—Doctora Cruz Barrancón—who was our eyes and ears in the government.

"Morse, thank God I got you. Listen, something terrible's happened. Cruzita is at the Health Ministry. Oil Minister Renaldo Brunesco was found dead just now. Poisoned, it looks like. The provincial capital buildings are locked down and she can't leave or call out. She sent one of her patients running over here to say that a squadron of federal troops are on their way to shut down the conference. The poor man was in tears."

"Someone poisoned Brunesco? When? Do any of the other staff at the conference know?"

"You had better round them up. I'm on my way over."

"Wait a second, Lotte. I don't think you should be here. Everyone knows that Brunesco was one of our harshest opponents. They need a scapegoat. This might even be a ruse just to bust us. I think you should stay away from here, and from the OCA office, for that matter. Poor Cruzita, she'll be a suspect, for sure."

"Of course. We should stay off the phones, too, so I have to come over. You, me, Cruzita, everyone, we're in this together."

"I guess we are. I'll leave word at the table how to reach me. Bye, darling. Be careful."

"You too. I love you."

I began to look for the staff in the crowded lobby and was lucky to see Rosa, a medical student with a good head on her shoulders. I waved and she came over.

"Rosa, we've got an emergency. In a few minutes, this place is going to be swarming with federal troops."

Her face lit up in a smile. "They're actually raiding us? Awesome!"

"No, no. Listen carefully. The oil minister has been murdered. I don't have to tell you this will be seen as a blessing for our movement, so everybody here is under suspicion. Round up a couple of other volunteers and get on the PA system. Explain the situation. Say that this is serious, that everybody has to stay calm and comply with official orders. Understand? Say something like this:

This is not a raid, not a persecution. The federales only want to know who's here. The officers will tell you what to do. Please don't start a confrontation. Please do as you are told. Give them true information, but only what you have to. You may leave now if you wish, but if you choose to stay, stay close together. Don't touch any soldier or any military equipment.

Don't run or make sudden moves. If you have something you should not be carrying, better get rid of it now.

"Like that. This crowd will understand. Tell them we're really sorry this has happened. You know I can't make myself conspicuous, but I won't disappear, I'll be around to help."

"Oh yes, Morse, I know that. I guess my group can handle this."

"Thanks, Rosa. Oh, and get someone to the press room. Tell them we're complying with orders. We need all the cameras we can get to focus on this. I'm going to try to find the rest of the staff now. Have you seen any of them?"

"Well, Massoud is emcee, he must be on or near the stage."

I nodded and she ran off. As soon as her voice came on the PA system, conversations around me stopped for a moment. An eerie quiet fell over the hallways, and we could hear the wail of sirens in the distance. Almost at once I heard people shouting: "Come on! Everyone to the auditorium!" and "Make signs, like this! Hold them up, so your group can find each other!" and "Come on, we've got to tell the people outside!" Everyone began to move quickly but without panic, some heading toward the auditorium, others toward the exits. The sirens fell silent a good distance from the conference center, and a line of military trucks soon filled the avenue in front of the auditorium. Troops in riot gear piled out and took up positions around the main buildings, while a group of officers and civilian authorities marched up the steps and into the lobby. The crowd spoke in low voices now. Where the hell was Massoud? And where was Lotte?

I shouldn't have worried. As I worked my way toward the podium, a lusty cheer went up from the crowd, and I saw our colleague Massoud bound up the steps to the stage. He waited for a moment, a calm, ironic smile on his dark Persian face, while a half-dozen government officials and army officers filed onto the stage after him, looking dour and uncomfortable. Cameras were flashing, TV units rolling.

"Good afternoon, everybody," Massoud began, and the crowd returned his greeting. "Thanks for your patience. I hope we can get on with our conference in a few hours. By now you've probably heard that there has been a terrible crime, that Oil Minister Renaldo Brunesco has tragically died, apparently at the hands of his enemies. Whatever we think of Señor Brunesco's policies, I'm sure you'll agree with me that violence never solves anything; it's against our way. So I know you'll agree with me, that it is now of the greatest importance to find those guilty of this crime and bring them to justice."

"If they can figure out what justice is!" called a woman's voice. There was a murmur of approval.

Massoud went on, unsmiling now. "The laws of Ecuador are just. I'm sure all of us will continue our work to make sure that they're followed exactly. Anyway, it's unfortunate that this happened during our conference, as the sudden presence of so many visitors in the city complicates the work of the investigators. As part of the investigation, all of us here at the conference have been asked to go through an identity check. I'm assured that the work of the police is limited to this one incident, and that no one here will be charged with any other infraction, as long as we comply with directions." He turned to one of the officers. "Here on my left is Major Eduardo Coroña, who will explain the details. Please give him and his colleagues your cooperation, with full courtesy. I understand that the situation is frustrating for all of us, but the quicker we get it done, the sooner we can get on with our program. Thank you." As he handed the mike to the colonel, Massoud's smile returned. "Solidaridad!" he yelled, and again the crowd answered, "Solidaridad! Solidaridad!" The major kept his dignity, though it seemed to me he was suppressing a smile of his own.

The inspection was much like intake at an immigration point. Tables were set up in the lobby, where participants were required to show their passport or domestic ID cards, give their addresses, be fingerprinted and photographed, and sign a statement they had no knowledge of the crime. Then they were handed a release slip that allowed them to pass through the exit point in the troop cordon around the building.

Everything seemed to go smoothly, but I cursed myself for being in this position. Lotte and I had false ID documents. Plainclothes police must have been watching the conference closely from the beginning, and they already knew who the organizers were. Trying to escape would only draw further attention to ourselves. The mere thought of being a refugee again exhausted me. I also worried about Massoud. Although he had committed no crime that I knew of, he was already a well-known source of irritation to the government. My only consolation was that the government had so many enemies we all might get lost in the shuffle.

As I inched forward in line, I saw that they were checking names against a list. I was sure to be on that list, I thought, and yes, the young soldier at the table handed my ID card to an MP who had a radio mic strapped to his head and a supply of plastic zip-tie handcuffs hanging from his belt. All my life I have had trouble dealing with this kind of senseless authority. I never advertise the fact that I am a professor, but to be treated like a common fool, a criminal, or a lunatic has always thrown me into an irrational rage. The sight of the soldier who was about to handcuff me made me furious, mad enough to fight. He instantly read this in my face and reached for his sidearm, shouting at the top of his lungs, "On the floor! Down, asshole!" Before he could level his weapon I charged at him, but he dodged me and landed a stinging blow to the side of my head with his pistol, and I went down. At once two other soldiers were on top of me, their knees in my back, their boots kicking me as I thrashed and swore on the ground. Before I knew it they had my arms twisted painfully behind my back and put the cuffs on, tight enough to hurt, then pulled me roughly to my feet and began to march me toward the doors. There, their way was blocked by a phalanx of students, but the MP were already speaking into their headsets, calling for backup. The sight of me with my bloody head stirred up the students and they stood their ground, screaming at the soldiers, until a dozen troops burst in from behind them, with nightsticks and pepper spray.

In the melee I somehow got pulled away from my captors. I felt myself yanked violently here and there in the riot, until suddenly I heard the distinctive snip of a nail clippers and felt my cuffs come off. As the chaos continued, a middle-aged man I had never seen before shoved my ID card and a release slip into my hand, spun me around, and pushed me in the direction of the exit point. No! I had to find Lotte and Massoud! I stopped and turned, but the stranger was gone, and in a second I was up against the wall, being handcuffed again, no doubt this time with the charge of resisting arrest. By now I was too exhausted to fight back, and as I looked around I saw students smiling, waving the peace sign, giving me the thumbs up, and my anger melted into elation. In the new world that was being born, everything would be an opportunity. Everything. A couple of dozen of the students who had resisted were under arrest too. As they marched us toward the van, I looked around and saw that many of us were smiling. No matter where we were, we would be as if together, and Lotte and Massoud and Cruzita too.

They censor my mail and reading material here, so I will not be able to follow events in the outside world, but I have learned how to get messages to and from Cruzita. As a Ministry of Health doctor, she has close friends in the prison dispensary, especially a male nurse named Eduardo, whose family are shamans in the mountains. To this end I often find myself with severe back pain, asthma, night sweats, and constipation—the last one a reality, thanks to a diet mostly of plantains, rice, and beans. The OCA office in Guayaquil is closed, but Lotte and the others have moved into the Sierra, where their work is thriving, it seems. I handwrite two copies of each page of this manuscript, and Eduardo smuggles out two or three pages at a time. I feel the dexterous hands of the *aroe,* the Tuatha de Danán, Yukichi's ancestors, and all the Druids and shamans living and dead, guiding my pen and protecting my words; and I know that these words have already secured the future of the old spirits' wisdom. In the language of so-called civilization, the struggle will be very, very long; but—as the Deep Code teaches us—duration is an illusion, and the future is here, now.